Nick's eyes burned into her soul

"We go well together, Olivia," he said thickly, and reaching for her, he pulled her to him. "I want you very badly."

Olivia swallowed, her cheeks hot and flushed. "But I don't want you. I don't want anything to do with you."

Nick's eyes darkened. "Don't lie," he muttered, catching her chin and tilting back her head. "You feel it, too."

She shook her head desperately. "No," she moaned, her voice low and throbbing.

"There's something between us. You felt it when I kissed you—you can't deny it. I almost went up in flames and so did you."

"But it isn't right, Nick," Olivia said breathlessly, closing her eyes to stop the sting of tears.

SARAH HOLLAND

deadly angel

Harlequin Books

TORONTO • NEW YORK • LOS ANGELES • LONDON
AMSTERDAM • PARIS • SYDNEY • HAMBURG
STOCKHOLM • ATHENS • TOKYO • MILAN

For
my mother

Harlequin Presents first edition March 1983
ISBN 0-373-10576-2

Original hardcover edition published in 1982
by Mills & Boon Limited

CHAPTER ONE

IT started at six o'clock in New York City.

Nick Baretta was relaxing in the oak-panelled board-room of his company. His crisp white shirt was loosened at the throat, and he leaned back with his feet on the table. He had only arrived back from Italy two days ago, and ever since then he had been besieged by his staff. He wearied of their inability to do anything with-out first consulting him. Where was their initiative, for God's sake?

He poured himself a stiff shot of whisky from the crystal decanter in front of him. The whisky hit the back of his throat, and he sighed, closing his eyes briefly. It was the first moment he had had to himself for two days, and he wasn't wasting it. Running a multi-million-dollar company single-handed was tiring in the extreme.

His heavy lids flickered open, his smoky grey eyes travelling over the stately boardroom for a moment. He smiled grimly. He was satisfied with his achievements, but a man who was satisfied was only half alive.

He champed at the bit, longing for the heady excite-ment of a new challenge, a new risk. It was all too easy now. All he had to do was snap his fingers and he got what he wanted immediately. Sometimes he wondered whether he would prefer being poor again, having the biting challenge of fighting his way to the top again.

He had clawed his way out of the gutter, trampling on anything or anyone who tried to get in his way. He had been ruthless, uncompromising, and in the end no one ever tried to stop him. Not ever. They valued their lives too much to cross swords with Nick Baretta.

He sighed wearily and ran a hand over his eyes. He was tired, but what had happened to him? Nothing but routine work. He wondered where all the excitement had gone. Did he want it back? But he knew the answer to that already.

Poverty was only romantic in storybooks. In reality it was harsh and dangerous, and the stench of it still lay heavy in his nostrils. The memories of New York's Little Italy cut deep into his soul; it was a jungle, and he knew he would kill rather than go back there.

His eyes narrowed as the telephone bell shrilled into the silence. He decided to ignore it, but it kept on ringing. With a muttered curse he reached out one tanned hand and snatched up the receiver.

'Yes?' he said curtly. Nothing was going to get him out of his private sanctuary. Or so he thought.

It only took two words. 'Greg's dying!' His mother's whispered voice made the room freeze into a chilling tableau.

An icy hand gripped his heart as he listened, his stomach tightening as though from a physical blow. He felt as though someone had just kicked his teeth in as he listened to her sobbing words.

Finally he spoke. 'Go to the hospital, Mamma,' he told her in a voice which was deep but shook just a fraction, 'I'll meet you there.' He replaced the receiver with icy precision.

He stared at the ceiling for a moment with unseeing grey eyes, then he drained his glass, slammed it on the polished mahogany table, picked up his jacket and strode from the room.

The streets of New York were against him. Traffic poured in a steady stream, and his knuckles showed white at the bone as he gripped the steering wheel.

His urgency made him careless, and he jumped a red light at the corner of Park Avenue. From behind him he saw the blue and white of a police car waving him over. 'Hell!' he muttered, complying angrily.

The policeman strode over to him with a self-important swagger, ready to haul him in, or at the very least tick him off. The electric window rolled down, and the policeman swallowed, visibly taken aback.

He stared for a moment, then said, 'Good evening, Mr Baretta,' his voice apologetic as he recognised the man behind the wheel. 'How are you?' He tilted his cap respectfully.

Nick's lips curled sardonically. 'I'm in a hurry.'

The policeman flushed a little. 'Can I give you an escort?'

Nick inclined his black head. 'Santa Teresa Hospital,' he told him, 'And make it fast!' The window rolled up swiftly and he re-started the engine.

Twenty minutes later, with sirens whirring and lights flashing, they arrived at the hospital entrance. Nick gave the officer a nod of thanks and strode into the building, making his way towards the emergency ward.

The pristine white walls were tainted with the smell of death and sickly disinfectant, the corridors echoing with the click-clack of nurses' feet. Nick felt physically sick as he stopped in front of a set of white doors, knowing who lay on the other side of them. He hesitated for a moment, then grimly pushed the doors apart with his long hands and strode into the room.

He stood in a frozen silence, staring at the face of his dying brother. He felt the anger harden his mouth, burning deep into his soul. Greg was too young, he hadn't lived. Twenty-six was no age to meet death.

He closed his eyes tightly on a spasm of pain, trying to shut out the anger that made him want to tear this room apart with his bare hands. Breathing deeply, he thought of the woman who had caused this—a cold-hearted English bitch who thought more of her model-girl looks than the life of a young man. The need for revenge ate into him and he clenched his fists.

He was a man who could neither forgive nor forget. His ancestry would not allow him to do so, nor would his personal feelings. He would find this English girl, and when he did, he would make her pay for what she had done to his brother.

'Nick!' A drawling Italian voice brought him out of his thoughts.

He turned, his smoky grey eyes flickering, still in the grip of his anger as he looked towards the door. 'What is it, Tonino?' he asked abruptly.

Tonino Corelli watched him with dark eyes that held the wisdom of one who has seen the world and all its evil, and keeps the memory locked inside. His face was carved on a slanting, heavy Roman bone structure, his dark hair falling around his face.

'He's awake,' Tonino said simply, his gaze switching to the young man on the bed.

Nick's head swung round, focusing on his brother. Slowly he walked over to the bed and stood over it, every line of his lean hard body held in tension.

'Hi!' Greg's voice was a threadbare whisper, his face almost a death-mask. His normally alive blue eyes were dull and lifeless as he looked up at his elder brother.

Nick kept his face harsh and expressionless. 'Why?' he asked point-blank, seeing no reason to waste time on idle talk. He needed to know if he was right, if the woman was behind it all.

Greg's face paled to a sickly white. 'I couldn't live without her,' he said, holding Nick's eyes for a second. He looked away a moment later, his gaze blank. 'She means everything to me.'

Nick's mouth firmed into an uncompromising line. He curbed his desire to comment on his brother's stupidity for getting mixed up with a woman like that. He looked down at him once more. 'You'll get better,' was all he said, and his voice carried the hard edge of conviction. He wouldn't allow his brother to die: it was as simple as that.

Greg looked round slowly, then his eyes met Nick's. 'Yes,' he murmured, seeing the grim determination on Nick's face.

Nick watched him for a moment longer, then turned away, walking back to Tonino. 'What did the doctor say?' he asked, sliding his hands into the pockets of his superbly tailored suit.

Tonino shrugged. 'He lost a lot of blood,' he told him, his accent a mixture of New York drawl and lilting Italian, 'but they pumped it back bit by bit. He'll pull through, eventually.'

The tension eased a little from Nick's body. He nodded briefly, relief evident on his hard-boned face. 'And the girl?'

Tonino held out a piece of paper in one slim hand. 'I got her address, boss.'

Nick took it, his eyes scanning it briefly. 'She lives in

London,' he murmured, his brows drawing in a frown.
He had thought she was living in New York, but obviously she had returned home. No doubt that was why
Greg had slit his wrists. He looked up at Tonino, the
grey eyes narrowing. 'You're sure it's the right address?'

'Sure.' Tonino spread his slim hands in a casual gesture, his long elegant body at ease as he studied Nick.

Nick slipped the piece of paper in his pocket. He
turned his head to study the motionless form of his
brother on the bed, and winced, running a hand over
his eyes. With a harsh sigh he said, 'Book me some tick-
ets on . . .'

'I already did, boss,' Tonino told him, concern etched
on to the deep-set eyes. He slid his hands into the
pockets of his double-breasted suit. 'You're on
Concorde in an hour. You'd better hurry.'

A grim smile touched Nick's mouth. His hand shook
as he ran it through his thick black hair. 'Tell Mamma I
had to leave quickly,' he said, his voice thickening.

Tonino nodded. 'Sure, boss.' He clapped a hand on
Nick's shoulder reassuringly. 'I'll think of something,
don't worry.'

Nick's grey eyes held his in silent thanks for a
moment. Then he took one look at Greg, and felt his
throat tighten with anger. He would recover, but at what
cost? He looked away.

'Hey,' he said, moving swiftly towards the door, 'get
me a car, will you, Tonino?'

He was coming for her.

Olivia was worried. She stood in the centre of the room,
a frown of concern etched into her brow as she thought
of Greg. He had slammed the telephone down on her

two hours ago, and ever since then she had been worried about him, filled with a gnawing sense of unrest.

He had been badly hurt, she knew that. She had tried to let him down gently so many times, but he hadn't allowed her to finish her sentences, and had cut her short, not wishing to hear what she had to say. It had made her all the more worried about breaking it off with him.

But even though he had been upset while she was still in New York, she had never heard quite the same note of desperation in his voice as she had just now. There had been a powerful urgency; something intangible, something so minor that she could not put her finger on it. But it had nagged at her since the moment she had first picked up the receiver.

She bit her lip, her slanting blue eyes focusing on the telephone. She could always ring him back, find out how he was. She sighed heavily, closing her eyes. It could give him fresh hope, re-kindle a spark of optimism which could never become a flame.

But anxiety got the better of her. She picked up the telephone, her long pale fingers dialling a number without hesitation.

'Baretta Incorporated, can I help you?' The voice came through loud and clear, the call being picked up on the third ring.

'Mr Greg Baretta, please,' Olivia told the telephonist, her fingers tracing the smooth dial absently.

'I'm sorry, Mr Greg left an hour ago,' the voice told her. 'Can I put you through to his secretary?'

Olivia's frown deepened. She bit her lip anxiously and shook her head. 'No,' she said slowly. 'No, I'll ring back some other time.' She replaced the receiver, feeling distinctly uncomfortable.

If only it could have ended some other way! She had been deeply fond of Greg, but he had forced the situation to a point where she had no choice but to be brutally honest with him.

She wished she knew how he was taking it. Badly, she realised with a grimace. She didn't know how badly.

The next evening, Olivia leaned back in the black leather seat of the taxi with a tired sigh. The modelling job that day had been back-breaking; the takes and re-takes, the outfit changes had all worn on her nerves. Her jaw was aching from constantly smiling into the fish-like eye of the camera.

She caught her reflection in the glass partition of the taxi. The long glossy black hair flowed over her shoulders, framing a heart-shaped, magnolia-white face, her lips full and pink, her cheekbones high and delicate. But it was her eyes that brought out her beauty. A bright, dazzling blue, they shone from her pale face like brilliant sapphires, glittering inside deep-set lids.

The full moon hung against the backcloth of night like a beautiful silver dollar. The street-lamps shone gold across the houses, picking out the wetness on the grey slate roofs. London was beautiful at night. It was good to be home, Olivia thought with a smile. New York had been exciting, but London was her home, and no one could forget their roots, however hard they might try.

'Here we are, love.' The taxi came to a halt, and the driver reached one hand back to open her door. Olivia stepped into the damp street, smelling the fresh night air, listening to the chugging of the engine as she paid the driver. She overtipped him because of her good mood, and he chuckled.

'Thank you very much, miss,' he said, eyeing the money in his palm. 'Must be the full moon—has a strange effect on people, so I'm told!'

Olivia smiled, turning to walk to her gate, but her eye was caught by a long black limousine parked on the other side of the road. Frowning, she wondered who it belonged to. It seemed very out of place in the cosy suburban street. Someone obviously had wealthy friends.

She walked up the path to the rambling old house which contained her flat, then some kind of premonition made her stop dead in her tracks just before she reached the door.

A slight breeze stirred the bushes gently, and Olivia's eyes narrowed as she searched the darkness for whatever it was she thought was there. She swallowed, making out a dark, tall shadow in the doorway of her flat.

'Who's there?' she asked loudly, hoping to scare off a potential rapist or mugger.

The only sound was that of the breeze against the leaves. Her heart beat a little faster with sudden fear as she peered into the darkness.

There was a leaping gold flame as a lighter flicked open. A face leapt out at her, illuminated by the flare of the lighter, and she stepped backwards, startled by the sinister features. She had a fleeting impression of steel-grey eyes, heavy-lidded, and a harsh face with chiselled bone structure. A strong, firm mouth clamped over the end of a cigar.

'It is Miss Courtney, isn't it?' a deep smoky voice asked. 'Miss Olivia Courtney?'

Common sense told her that if he knew her name, he wasn't likely to be a prospective rapist. He would surely have attacked her by now if he was.

'What do you want?' she asked, brushing his question aside.

There was a pause, then he stepped out of the shadows. Gold ran along his angular cheekbones as the light flashed on to his face, the full moon glinting on his raven-black hair, his eyes for a moment silver.

'I want you, Miss Courtney,' he drawled.

Olivia stayed where she was, afraid to move in case he followed. 'If it's about an assignment,' she said briskly to cover up her nerves, 'I suggest you make an appointment with my agent.'

The man smiled, and Olivia's blood ran cold. 'I wanted to inspect the goods myself,' he drawled.

She stiffened at his tone, her lips tightening. 'And how do you find them?'

His gaze flicked slowly over her slender curves, sliding back to her face to trace the pale white skin framed by glossy black hair, and finally resting on her brilliant, dazzling blue eyes.

'Adequate,' he drawled.

Her eyes sparkled with sudden anger. She tried to push past him, but his powerful body blocked her path. 'Excuse me,' she said tightly, not looking at him.

A hand closed around her wrist. 'I want to talk to you,' he said coldly, and Olivia had the impression that he had been playing a game up till then, which he had now tired of playing.

'What about?' she asked, avoiding his gaze.

'A mutual friend.' He glanced towards the door, his face expressionless. 'Shall we go inside?'

She looked up slowly, her eyes tracing the harsh angularity of profile. 'You're nothing to do with modelling, are you?' she asked, and felt the first stirrings of real unease, her body held stiffly as she looked at him, her stomach tightened in anticipation. 'Who are you? And how did you know my address?'

His smile was chilling. 'Oh, I know all about you, Miss Courtney,' he drawled, and a frisson of alarm ran down her spine.

There was a brief silence. Then she said in a low voice, 'Who are you?'

The grey eyes held hers. 'My name is Baretta—Nick Baretta.'

Her heart stopped for a fraction of a second as she stared at him in sheer disbelief. Her eyes had widened, dazzling the eye with their brilliant blue, now even stronger against the pale moonlit curve of her cheek.

'Greg's brother?' she asked through dry lips.

He inclined his black head. 'You didn't notice the family resemblance?' His voice was cold, mocking.

She threw him a sharp angry look. 'It isn't very strong.'

He looked nothing like Greg. Greg was charming, lighthearted, going through life laughing at everything he met. It showed on his face; smooth, unlined by experience, he looked much younger than his years.

But Nick's face carried the harsh reality of his childhood. Every line on that tanned face showed the ruthlessness with which he had scrambled out of the gutter, to become one of the wealthiest and most feared men in the world.

'Why are you here?' she asked him suddenly. 'Is it something to do with Greg?' She held her breath, worry making her brow crease with a frown. 'Tell me what's happened!'

'Do you care?' he asked harshly.

'Of course!' Her frown deepened, perplexed.

'I'd rather discuss it inside,' he told her in a cold voice, his eyes flicking towards the pale green wooden door.

Olivia hesitated, then realised he wasn't going to go away if she didn't let him in. Nick followed her in silently, with the tread of a wolf, and she looked at the flat through his eyes.

The fat cosy armchairs dominated the room, their flowery pattern giving the room a summer feel, bright and warm. Most of her friends were surprised by her home, expecting to find something with more glamour. But although she did a glamorous job, she didn't want to be surrounded by it all the time. The only glamour attached to her work was the finished product, and that was only accomplished by back-breaking work. Besides, she couldn't relax among silk and velvet.

She eyed Nick as she stood in the centre of the room, her face angry but controlled. 'Do you always take women by surprise like that?' she asked.

'No,' he drawled, 'I usually just take them.'

Her face flushed a little at his words, her mouth tightened. 'I'd be grateful if you didn't take too long. I have to be up early in the morning.'

'Working?' he asked, his voice icy. 'It comes first with you all the way, doesn't it?'

Her eyes flashed bright blue. 'I have to earn a living!'

'While my brother is dying!' His voice bit like a whip-lash and she fell silent in frozen horror, staring at him as her entire world seemed to focus on his face. He studied her with hard grey eyes. 'Didn't you know?'

'No,' she whispered, her throat tight, her eyes wide with shock. She was frozen to the spot, her body held in ice.

Nick drew on his cigar, smoke curling silently in a

silver-blue ribbon. 'You discard people like tissues once they've outlived their relevance,' he said. 'I doubt if you've given a thought to my brother since you came back from New York. While he's thought of nothing else but you.'

'That isn't true!' she denied, trembling. 'I tried to . . .'

'Cut it out!' he said bitingly. 'You got rid of Greg the minute you had a new contract in London. You didn't give a damn whether you broke his stupid infatuated little heart.' His upper lip curled in a sneer. 'All you were interested in was your precious career!'

'I was very fond of him,' she said shakily, her face white.

'Like hell!' Nick muttered through his teeth, and the violence in his tone silenced her. There was a brief tense pause, then he said, 'Miss Courtney, my brother took a razor and slit his wrists open last night.'

Olivia stared in shock, an icy hand gripping her heart. Her face paled to a deathly white, her mouth parting as she looked at him in a stunned silence. Her mind flashed a brief, sickened image of Greg, his blood flowing out of his wrists on to white sheets, and she winced, pushing it away, her stomach tightening.

She held his eyes. 'Is he all right?' she whispered through pale lips, refusing to admit that Greg could be dying.

Nick studied her for a moment. 'He's recovering,' he said tersely. He slid his hands into his pockets, watching as she sat heavily in a chair, her hands pressed against her hot cheeks.

'I had no idea,' she said, shaking her head in disbelief. 'If I'd known he'd tried to kill himself, I would have . . .'

'Yes?' he cut in sardonically. 'You would have what? Flown out to be by his side?' His mouth crooked cynically. 'How touching! But I can't picture it somehow. Can you?'

She felt her mouth tremble at his harsh words. She had been deeply fond of Greg. How dared this man come here and judge her when he knew nothing whatsoever about her?

Controlling her anger with him, she asked, 'Why did he do it?'

'Oh, come now, Miss Courtney.' His tone was biting, cynical. 'You don't expect me to believe you have no idea why he should want to die?' His gaze flicked over her, the steel grey eyes icy.

Olivia knew deep down why he had done it, but she had to be told to believe it. 'I don't,' she said angrily, 'or I wouldn't be asking you.'

'He was crazy about you and you knew it,' he muttered between tightly clenched teeth, 'but that didn't bother you, did it? You dumped him without a thought and came home to England.'

She bit her lower lip. It hurt to hear it. 'I tried to tell him it was over so many times,' she said blankly, 'but he just wouldn't listen to me.'

Nick straightened, his face tight. 'It makes very little difference now,' he pointed out, studying her. He paused, then turned his head, his gaze scanning the room. 'How long will it take you to pack?'

Olivia looked up at his question, her brow marring with a frown. 'What?' She didn't think she had heard properly. Perhaps shock was making her hear things.

'I asked you how long it would take to pack.'

That was what she thought he had said. Her frown

deepened as she watched him, her eyes narrowing. 'Why should I want to pack?'

There was a brief silence as they looked at each other, and Olivia could hear her heart beating with shock, thudding out a slow, heavy rhythm against her breastbone.

'You're coming to New York.'

She shook her head. 'I can't—I've just signed a deal with Montoux for the next month at least.' Biting her lip, she frowned. 'I don't think I can get out of it.' Alistair would kill her if she tried to. He was her agent, and he had taken a long time to set the deal up.

'You'll have to try,' Nick told her in a clipped tone. 'We leave on the afternoon flight tomorrow.'

Olivia's mouth compressed. 'What's the mattter with you?' she demanded, irritation at his arrogance making her angry. 'I've just told you—I can't leave at such short notice!'

The grey eyes narrowed. 'I'll handle it. Just make sure you're ready by lunchtime tomorrow.' He took a step towards her, his face threatening. 'If you're not, I'll come and find you.'

Olivia stood up, her face angry. 'If I walk out on them now, I'll never get another job.' Models had to be professional, had to do as they were told—especially if they weren't big names. If she walked out on Montoux, they would have her blacklisted.

'Too bad.' His biting tone was not in the least sympathetic. 'If it was left to me, I'd have you strangled, but my brother's survival is obviously dependent on you. He needs you to get well again, and I'm here to see that he gets what he needs.'

Anger made her forget Greg for a split second. 'You

swine!' she snapped, her fists clenching at her sides. 'You can't force me to go against my will!'

His smile was chilling. 'Can't I?' He ran his eyes over her slowly. 'I'm sure you'll find my methods very persuasive. You're coming if I have to drag you all the way there.'

There was an intense silence. 'You wouldn't dare!' she said through tight lips.

'Oh, I'd dare, Miss Courtney,' he said in a menacing sinister voice. 'But I advise you not to challenge me. Not ever.'

She shivered, as though someone had just trickled icy water down her spine. Unable to reply, she stared at him with furious rage, her face tightening as she controlled the need to hit out at him.

Nick turned, his lithe, muscular body fitting perfectly in the black dinner suit he wore. 'Goodnight,' he said, turning his head to look at her over his shoulder. 'Until twelve tomorrow.'

Olivia hurled a little china ornament at the door, watching in helpless rage as the china smashed into little fragments, splintering as the crash echoed through the empty flat. Outside came the roar of a powerful engine as Nick Baretta drove off into the night.

She sank down on to the chair, her face in her hands as she closed her eyes tightly. Poor Greg, she thought, her heart wincing. She had known something was wrong, had sensed it, as though some sixth sense had been warning her of his desperation.

Meeting his brother had been a shock to her. She had heard about Nick, of course—who hadn't? But Greg had spoken of him in tones that suggested both hero-worship and a good friendship. She had expected someone strong, but someone more like Greg.

Nothing could have prepared her for the impact of Nick Baretta himself. His face held the stamp of ruthlessness, his lean body holding a threat of sexual violence which made her stomach clench in fear and excitement. He was a dangerous, powerful man.

She hardly slept that night. The two brothers kept her awake, pushing through her mind while she tossed and turned in her bed. Each had had a searing impact on her; Greg lying in a hospital bed made her want to cry out loud at the futility of his actions, Nick's hostile arrogance made her want to cry louder with rage.

It wasn't until dawn spread her lazy golden fingers over London that she fell asleep. She was woken at nine-thirty by the traffic which flowed noisily past her flat. She scrambled out of bed, gasping at the time. She had to go to the bank, see Alistair, and visit her sister before leaving for New York.

The chic black dress she wore rippled beneath the camelhair coat which fitted her body exquisitely. A long, pure silk white scarf flowed around her neck, its delicate fringes rippling in the London breeze.

The men on a building site opposite Alistair's office whistled to her. Olivia gave them a little smile over her shoulder as she pushed the glass door back and walked into the building that housed the agency. Fickle! she thought with a smile as she heard them whistle to another girl a moment later.

Alistair's outer office was in chaos. Plants were dying on the windowsill, papers heaped higgledy-piggledy on the desk, a wastepaper bin on the floor overflowed with paper cups.

The door of his office opened. 'You!' exclaimed Alistair, looming in the doorway with an air of agitation. 'In here!'

Alistair Frobisher was a man who lived on electric wires. He was thin and energetic, his fingers always busy, clicking restlessly, rapping on desks, linking and unlinking, playing with pens. He was tall and lanky, with a riot of unmanageable curly orange hair, his face bony, the cheeks hollowed by years of running around without eating, his nervous tension eating up everything he put inside himself.

'I've just had a phone call,' he told her ominously, rapping his long thin fingers on the desk, and watched her sit down gracefully opposite him.

'Really?' she murmured, unbuttoning her coat slowly and crossing her long, slim legs. She wasn't at all surprised. She could guess who the other call had been from.

'In fact,' said Alistair, his beady eyes darting over her, 'I've just had two.' He raised his hand and began counting vigorously on his fingers. 'One from Montoux—who, I might add, are absolutely climbing the walls!'

Olivia sighed deeply. 'I know,' she said, looking at her hands, her mouth pursed. 'I can guess who the other call was from.'

He started playing with a black pen, upending it restlessly. 'Nick Baretta,' he said quickly, watching her. He threw the pen down irritably. 'Nick Baretta, for God's sake! What the hell are you doing, Olivia? Do you realise who this guy is?'

She nodded. 'He's Nick Baretta,' she said solemnly.

Alistair. was not amused. 'Ho, ho,' he said, leaning back and twiddling his bony fingers together. 'He's a dangerous guy to be playing around with. How the hell did you catch his attention?'

Olivia sighed and shrugged. She looked over at the dirty blinds over the office window. 'I don't. know,' she murmured, frowning. A pneumatic drill began making a hideous noise on the building site and set her teeth on edge. 'He just sort of burst in and announced that I was going to New York.'

Alistair gave a short crack of laughter. 'I can imagine.' He began pacing up and down the office, and Olivia wondered how long it would be before he had a heart attack; he always seemed just on the verge of one. 'You realise we're going to lose thousands because of this?' He came to stand in front of her, his hands fidgeting at his sides. 'This was the biggest deal we've had!'

Olivia eyed him. 'I'm sorry,' she said, and sighed, running a hand through her glossy black hair. 'I did try to tell him, but he wasn't interested.'

'No,' Alistair said drily, and gave a heavy sigh, 'he wouldn't be. He practically owns everything he touches. The man's a walking Midas!' There was a trace of bitterness in his voice.

She looked at him sharply. 'Is anything wrong?' she asked worriedly, sensing more than usual distress behind his agitation. 'You seem more on edge than usual.'

He gave her a tight smile. 'Walking on coals, darling,' he said irritably. 'I thought we'd clinched it with Montoux, but . . .' he looked at her and shrugged wiry shoulders, 'well, anyway, you run along, I've got work to do.'

She stood up slowly, buttoning her camelhair coat and running her fingers over the thick pure silk scarf around her neck. 'Are you sure you're not in any kind of trouble?' she asked, frowning.

'No, no,' he assured her, hustling her out of the office. 'You run along to your Nick Baretta. I've got a pretty big meeting on. Besides,' he gave her a smile which was faintly crooked, 'Mr Baretta sounded pretty icy on the phone. I wouldn't want to tangle with him by making you late.'

She tightened her pale lips at the way her life was being quickly organised by Nick. 'Take care.' She leaned over and kissed Alistair's cheek, feeling the rough stubble on his chin. 'See you when I get back.'

The cool spring breeze outside the offices hit her unnoticed. Her mind was on Alistair. Was there something wrong with the agency? He had seemed very worried about something.

She walked slowly, unaware of the traffic that poured noisily around her, unaware of the other pedestrians who walked quickly, their hands thrust into their pockets as they made their way to their own destinations. She walked to the side of the road and began to cross.

A loud blast from a horn made her jump back on to the pavement, her heart thudding. She sighed. Nick Baretta was playing havoc with her nerves and her mind. She had almost walked in front of a car because of her occupied thoughts.

She pushed him from her mind and moved determinedly to the big blue bank on the corner of the road.

CHAPTER TWO

THE bank was crowded when she went in, and she waited impatiently behind a lady in a green coat who appeared to be telling the cashier her life story. With relief she finally went, and Olivia hurriedly got some cash out and put it in her black leather wallet, stuffing the notes in haphazardly.

She hailed a taxi, jumping in the back and saying quickly, 'Pimlico, please,' before the wheels moved and they crossed the traffic lights, speeding towards her sister's flat.

The doorbell rang for ages before it was finally answered. Olivia looked round as the black peeling door was opened a crack, and she smiled brightly at her sister.

'Hallo, Caroline,' she said, tilting her head. 'Can I come in?'

'Oh!' Caroline's sharp, pointed face peered at her through the crack, her eyes a sleepy blue, her black hair pulled back off her face. 'It's you!'

Caroline was a nightbird. She was dead during day-light hours, only coming alive in the evenings. Her face wore the pallor of someone who rarely gets fresh air, someone who sleeps through the day.

Olivia followed Caroline in, waiting while she leafed through a pile of letters on top of the electricity meter in the empty communal hall. 'None for me, as usual,' said Caroline with disgust, going back into her flat.

Olivia closed the door behind her, the dead silence in the flat ringing in her ears. 'I can't stay long,' she told her, slipping her hands in her coat pockets, 'I have to be home in about half an hour.'

'All right,' said Caroline, totally uninterested. She wore a dressing gown that had seen better days, the edges frayed, the waist sagging around her slim figure. 'Want some coffee?' She walked into the kitchen.

Olivia shook her head. 'Tea, please. But it'll have to be quick—I can't be late.'

Caroline frowned, looking at her elder sister properly for the first time. 'You're in a hurry,' she said curiously, plugging in the kettle and sniffling a little. 'What's the rush? Are you modelling today?'

Olivia perched on one of the sparse kitchen stools. 'No,' she said, watching her sister rub one hand tiredly over her eyes, 'I'm going back to the States. That's what I came to tell you.'

Caroline's brows rose, her face scrubbed clean of make-up. 'I thought that was all finished? You only just got back the other day.'

Olivia nodded. 'Well,' she said wryly, 'I'm going back. It's very complicated, so I shan't go into it.'

'No,' Caroline drawled, her mouth curving in a smile as she handed her some tea, 'I probably wouldn't take it all in anyway. It's too early in the morning for thinking.'

Olivia drank her tea quickly. She hadn't packed her things yet, she realised with dismay. She would have to get back to her own flat as soon as possible. Caroline wasn't particularly bothered that she was going back to New York. Olivia had just felt the need to tell someone where she would be. Nick Baretta worried her. She didn't want to think she was alone with him where no one knew where she was.

As she walked to the front door with Caroline, she heard movements in another part of the flat and looked at her sister quizzically.

'Mind your own business,' Caroline warned, opening the door and pushing her sister out with a nudge.

Olivia raised her brows. 'I will.' She waved as she walked down the path, and watched her sister close the door behind her with a click. Olivia sighed, her eyes scanning the road for a taxi.

As she drove back to her own flat, she felt her nerves begin to tighten. It was getting close to time now. Nick would be there at twelve, he had said, and it was now half past eleven. She bit her lip anxiously, wishing the London traffic would clear.

As she stepped out of the taxi, she caught sight of a long black limousine waiting silently outside her flat. Her heart twisted strangely as she saw it, and her pale mouth compressed. He was waiting for her.

The door of the sinister limousine clicked open, the chrome flashing in the spring sunlight, and Nick Baretta stepped out slowly on to the pavement.

'Where have you been?' he asked in a smoky voice, and his grey eyes ran over her slowly. 'I was beginning to think you'd run away like a little rabbit.'

Olivia stiffened, her mouth tightening. 'I had some things to attend to,' she said, walking to the gate which led to her flat.

Nick followed her, his pace lazy, unhurried. 'Nothing too serious, I hope,' he drawled. He was wearing a dark suit, the waistcoat emphasising his tight stomach and slim hips. A black cashmere overcoat gave him an air of power and wealth.

Olivia slipped her key in the lock and opened the door. She went into the flat, and he followed her with a silent tread. She heard the door close with a quiet click behind him, and looked round. 'I went to see my sister, if you must know,' she told him.

He was leaning against the door. 'Ah yes,' he drawled, watching her with steel-grey eyes, his heavy lids hooded, the long sooty black lashes flickering against his angular cheekbones. 'Caroline.'

Olivia felt her lips tighten. 'Know your stuff, don't you?' she said tightly.

Nick gave her a slow, chilling smile, but did not reply. She felt the hair on the back of her neck prickle, and she shivered. Watching him across the living room, she wondered how much he knew about her, and how he had found it out. Had Greg told him? She doubted that.

'I'll just pack,' she said coolly, turning to walk towards her bedroom door. 'I won't be long, if you'd like to wait here.'

His mouth crooked sardonically, his eyes flicking to the bedroom. 'Can't I come with you?' he murmured smokily, and his gaze roved over her with insolent appraisal until she stiffened, a frisson of alarm and anger running down her spine.

'No, you cannot,' she snapped through pale lips, and went into the other room, closing the door behind her. She hauled out her suitcase and slammed it on the bed, taking her clothes out of the wardrobe.

She looked in the mirror, seeing the angry flush on her cheeks, the way her eyes glittered with irritation. He was getting to her already. She would have to make sure she acted cool and controlled in future. It was the only way to handle a man like him.

Her heart stopped momentarily. Could she handle him?

They arrived in New York at one o'clock, the tyres of the aircraft screeching in protest as they bounced along the runway. Olivia was tense as she stepped off the glittering white plane and, through Customs and Immigration, walked beside Nick to the long menacing limousine that waited for them outside.

They were greeted by a dark Italian. He had an intense, serious face, his eyes dark, his bones slanting, carved on a Roman structure with an aquiline nose and a thin mouth.

'Tonino!' Nick greeted the man with a smile. He slid his hands in his pockets, studying him from beneath hooded lids, his body totally still for a moment. 'How is he?' he asked deeply, and Olivia saw the concern in his eyes.

Tonino's face broke into a grin, his features lighting up like a monkey's. 'He's doing good, boss,' he assured him in an Italian drawl. 'I saw him just before we left, and he looked okay.' He studied Nick's face, and grinned further. 'No, really, is true! He's getting better.'

They were obviously talking about Greg, and Olivia breathed a sigh of relief at the news. She gave the man a shy smile, looking through her lashes uncertainly. 'Hello,' she said in a quiet voice, 'I'm Olivia.'

Tonino looked at her with those dark eyes. 'Oh,' he said, his face uncertain for a moment. Then he gave her a brief nod. 'Hello.'

She flushed, realising he blamed her too. They drove

across the freeway to Manhattan, crossing Triboro
Bridge over the East River, the calm spring sunshine
lilting on the dappled water. Olivia watched the streets
flash by, and bit her lip, thinking of Greg. She was
anxious to see him.

The streets were grey and grimy, the neighbourhood
similar to the East End as they sped towards the centre
of the city. The pulse grew stronger as they veered
uptown, joining the snarling traffic, the horns blasting,
the sun glinting off roofs and windows vividly.

She looked sideways at Nick. 'When can I see Greg?'

'Such touching concern,' he drawled smokily, looking
across to her with a mocking smile, 'but a little late,
don't you think? This is the first time you've shown any
interest in him.' He arched one black brow. 'Why do I
get the feeling there's an ulterior motive behind it?'

That wasn't fair. Olivia tightened her lips and looked
away. She had only kept silent on the subject of Greg
because he had acted so arrogantly at first. She didn't
reply because she saw no point. He would let her see
Greg when he was ready. She frowned, wondering how
he was. The visions she kept having of him were terribly
upsetting, especially as she knew he'd tried to kill himself
for her. It was a terrible thing to have hanging over
your head.

They pulled up smoothly, and Olivia looked up at a
tall white building. Her eyes scanned the front of it,
seeing a sign which read: Santa Teresa Hospital. So they
had come straight to the hospital.

She wanted to ask why Nick hadn't told her they were
coming straight here. But what was the point, she
thought irritably, he'd only give her one of those slow,
icy smiles.

The afternoon sun glinted on the tall spikes of the buildings around them. 'Coming?' Nick drawled, opening her door and watching as she stepped out. The pace of the city drummed into her veins, the noisy streets, the free, open skyscrapers that touched the pale blue sky a direct combination.

Her nerves tightened as they walked side by side through the hospital, their heels clicking, making her nerves jangle. She closed her eyes briefly, hoping Greg was out of the danger area.

'He's in here.' Nick stopped in front of some white doors. His face was impassive, but she detected lines of strain around that firm mouth, around the smoky grey eyes. He was suffering as much as she, if not more. 'Act normally, don't upset him.'

She frowned. 'Of course I won't!'

'So long as you understand me. You're here to play the loving woman—holding his hand, smiling at him.' His gaze froze her where she stood. 'Play it any other way, and you'll make me very, very angry,' he added succinctly.

Olivia nodded, her throat tight. Then Nick pushed the doors apart and she walked inside.

She stopped dead, her heart contracting as she saw Greg, pale and sickly, in the stark white bed. Biting her lip, she walked slowly towards him. His lids flickered open as though he sensed her presence, and she was shocked by the pale lifeless blue of his eyes.

'Olivia!' He stared in disbelief as she came to sit by his side. 'Are you really here?' His pale hand reached out to clutch hers, and his white face broke into a smile. 'They told me you were coming, but I couldn't believe it—I thought you didn't care.'

She felt tears prick the back of her eyes. 'Of course I care, silly,' she said, cursing herself for hurting him so badly. Her eyes strayed to the white bandages around his wrists and she winced, unable to think of his self-inflicted injury.

A weak frown crossed his brow. 'But you went away,' he murmured. 'You told me you were never coming back.'

She brushed his hair with one hand, smoothing back the fine strands of dark brown that fell over his forehead. 'Sssh, Greg,' she told him, 'don't upset yourself. I'm here now, and I'm not going to go away again.' Until you're better, she added to herself. As soon as he was well, the best thing would be to go as far away as she could, and let him get over her on his own.

Greg squeezed her hand and smiled. He turned to look at Nick, who was standing on the other side of the bed. 'Hi, Nick,' he said weakly. 'Where have you been? I haven't seen you since that first night.'

Nick's mouth indented, his gaze meeting Olivia's. 'Someone tried to wriggle out of a deal,' he said with irony, and Olivia flushed. 'I had to persuade them not to.'

Greg was unaware of the undercurrents running between them. 'Have you seen Mamma yet?' he asked, his voice throaty.

Nick shook his head. 'I left in a hurry. I'll drop in on her this afternoon.'

Greg relaxed, his head sinking back on to the pillows with a contented sigh. 'I'm so glad you came,' he told Olivia happily, and she felt the tears sting her lids. 'Don't cry!' Greg said, misinterpreting them. He traced her cheek with one weak hand. 'I'll be better soon, and then we can get married.'

Olivia looked slowly across at Nick. His face was grim as he returned her gaze.

They left the hospital an hour later. Olivia was lost in her thoughts as she slipped into the black limousine beside Nick. He leaned forward and rapped on the glass partition. 'Okay, Tonino.'

The engine purred and they pulled away smoothly. Olivia sat back against the comfortable seat, her mind wandering. Greg had looked so weak, so lifeless. When she thought of the young man she had met when she first arrived in New York, it made her want to cry at the change in him.

They had been introduced at a party. It was her first week in the city, and she had felt lonely, needing a friend, someone to talk to and cheer her up. Greg had wandered over with a cheeky smile, and within minutes she was laughing at his jokes, listening to his amusing stories. She took to him immediately. But she didn't fall in love with him. It wasn't until she had been seeing him regularly for a month that she realised he was in love with her.

She had tried to break it gently, let him know she could never feel that way about him. But Greg had been confused, hurt, his eyes looking so much like a bewildered spaniel that her heart had ached for him with compassion.

'Just until you leave,' he had kept saying, his voice pleading, his eyes holding hers, so she had given in, unsure as to what she could possibly do on the face of his opposition.

She had never dreamed he would try to kill himself. She had had to come back to London, because the modelling assignment that had taken her to the States had finished, and she had nowhere to live and no money to live on. As she didn't intend to marry Greg, she could hardly stay in the city with him.

So she had come home. Greg rang her constantly, and within a week of her return they had had an icy row over the telephone. It was after that argument that he had presumably attempted suicide. She had told him point-blank that she wouldn't marry him. He had slammed the telephone down, and that was the last she had heard of him until now.

'Day-dreaming?' a dark smoky voice brought her out of her thoughts, and her head swung round.

'Oh,' she said, realising the car had stopped outside a tall block of apartment buildings. 'Sorry, I was thinking.'

A smile touched Nick's mouth. 'So I see,' he said, getting out of the car and coming round to help her out.

Olivia followed him into the luxuriously furnished entrance. 'Is this where you live?' Her voice was surprised as she scanned the foyer, taking in the silent exclusivity of their surroundings. She hadn't realised places like this existed.

They took the lift up to the top floor and stepped out into a penthouse suite. She held her breath at the taste and style of the room they went into—thick pale beige carpets, with elegant decor, it had a simplicity of line and colour that was beautiful.

'Drink?' Nick closed the door behind them and walked over to a cocktail cabinet.

She followed slowly. 'No, thank you. Do you live here alone?'

Nick's black head turned, his eyes narrowing. 'Now why should that interest you?'

She shrugged. 'Just curious.' She strolled over to the long windows at the end of the room, looking down on the streets below. The symphony of traffic was silenced by the thick panes of glass, but the cars moved erratically below, like millions of busy ants.

Olivia wondered when Nick would take her to her hotel, and was about to ask him when the door clicked open behind them and Tonino came into the room holding her case.

'Where shall I put it, boss?' he asked, holding it in the air with a smile.

Nick's eyes flicked to Olivia. 'In the bedroom,' he said softly, and his eyes mocked her.

She felt her pale mouth compress, her eyes sparkling. 'I'm not staying here with you!' she told him, watching angrily as Tonino went to a door on the other side of the room and put her case inside.

'No?' One dark brow rose.

'No!'

He laughed deep in his throat. 'Such beautiful eyes when you're angry,' he murmured, studying her with amusement. 'You know, you're a very attractive woman, Miss Courtney.' His gaze was insolent as it roamed over her body. 'I can see why my brother wanted you so badly.'

'Don't try to change the subject,' she said tautly, struggling to control her temper. 'I will not stay here alone with you. I want to be moved to a hotel immediately!'

His brows rose. 'I want you here where I can keep an eye on you.' He shrugged his powerful shoulders encased in a black jacket. 'I don't trust you. How do I know you wouldn't try to get back to London? No, Miss Courtney, you're not going anywhere.'

'You can't force me to stay here!'

'Can't I?' His face hardened as he watched her in a brief silence. Then he said, 'I advise you not to underestimate me. I make a point of getting what I want.'

She eyed him bitterly. 'By fair means or foul.'

He inclined his black head. 'Exactly.' He reached inside his jacket pocket, and she watched him as he lit a cigar, the silver-blue tendrils of smoke curling around his face. 'Don't worry,' he said, catching the tense rigidity of her body, 'I shan't expect to share your bed.'

She flushed angrily because he had guessed her thoughts so well. 'I'd rather share it with a rattlesnake!' she snapped, her hands clenching into fists.

'Oh, I'm far more deadly than a rattlesnake,' he drawled, and her blood ran cold.

She bit back a swift retort, watching him with angry blue eyes, her cool beautiful face tightly controlled. Common sense told her that the only course open to her was to wait until she had the chance, then slip away to a hotel. It was ludicrous to believe he could keep her here against her will.

Nick drew on his cigar, his eyes narrowed against the smoke. 'I'm driving to the Village now, to see my mother. I won't be long—I expect to be back at eight or so.'

She looked up sharply, feeling a glimmer of hope. Trying to conceal her excitement, she acted casually. 'Oh?' she said, her brows rising with what she hoped would pass for idle curiosity. If he left her here, she could take her chance and get away.

'Don't go anywhere, will you?' he murmured, and she thought she detected amusement in his gaze. 'I intend to take you out to dinner when I get back.'

That didn't matter now, because she would be gone by the time he got back. She smiled a little. 'I'll be here,' she said, lying in her teeth. With any luck she would be a million miles from him.

Nick's mouth curled in a smile. 'Good,' he said, and nodded at Tonino, who came forward to stand next to her. 'Tonino will look after you,' he said softly, his expression amused as he saw the irritation and defeat cross her features.

Tonino looked down at her with dark eyes. 'I'll see to it, boss.' He gave Olivia a mischievous smile. 'I'm good company,' he assured her, and she glared at him.

Nick laughed softly under his breath. 'He's my right-hand man,' he told her, and his eyes laughed at her. 'You'll be in good hands.' He ran one long finger down her cheek. *'Ciao,'* he said huskily.

Olivia watched as he walked out of the apartment, leaving her alone with Tonino Corelli. He slid his hands in his pockets, his dark head tilted to one side.

'Want to watch television?' he asked with a smile.

Olivia decided her best course was to be pleasant to him. 'No, thank you, Tonino.' Her eyes slid towards the door of her bedroom and she turned back to him with a quick smile. 'I think I'll rest for a while.'

He nodded sagely. 'Sure. Jet-lag is tiring, I know.'

She went across the room slowly and opened the door he had put her case into. As she took one last look at him he was walking over to the television set and switching it on. Olivia closed the door, leaning against it with a grim smile.

That, she decided, was the last she would see of Mr Corelli. Quickly, she went over to the bed and looked in her suitcase. It was too heavy to bother carrying downstairs—she might get caught because of its weight. If she just took her handbag with her she could use her credit card to pay any bills at the hotel. She grimaced, thinking of her rather sparse account. But it couldn't be helped. She had to stay somewhere, and she certainly wasn't going to stay here.

With great stealth, she went through the other door of her bedroom, which led into a long, thickly carpeted corridor. Creeping along on tiptoe, she felt a wild giggle rise inside her; she felt like Secret Squirrel. The only trouble was, her predicament was not particularly funny.

The corridor led into a hall, which led to the lifts, and she bit her lip as the lift arrived, hoping Tonino wouldn't hear it from the living room. She sagged against the wall, sighing with relief as the lift took her downstairs. Thank God for that, she thought, watching the red numbers mark her descent. It had been a lot easier than she had thought. She felt a little guilty because Tonino would no doubt be hanged for letting her get away. But she shrugged, trying to be logical; it was either him or her, she thought grimly.

The doors slid open and she groaned in disbelief as she saw Tonino lounging against the wall of the foyer. He strolled towards her, his wise, dark face calm.

'You might have saved me the trouble,' she said irritably as he put her back in the lift and pressed the little white button. The doors slid shut once more.

He spread his hands apologetically. 'Is not my fault,' he told her in his drawling accent. 'Nick knew you'd try and make a run for it. He just wanted to be sure.'

Olivia sighed, glancing at him across the lift. 'So you gave me the rope and watched me hang myself.' She was very annoyed—it had all been a deliberate ploy to see what she would do. She had played right into Nick's hands, and she was *not* looking forward to seeing him when he got back.

Tonino frowned. 'No really, is not like that,' he told her, his brow marked with deep thought. 'Is to see if he can trust you, that's all.' He watched her as the lift stopped and she stepped out with a defeated set to her shoulders. They walked into the suite, going through the door to the living room.

'It should have been obvious that I'd try to leave,' she pointed out to him as she put her bag down on the couch. 'After all, I don't even know him.'

He looked at her strangely. 'No, you don't, do you?'

Something in the tone of his voice made her frown, looking back at him with her head tilted to one side. 'Why do you say that?' she asked, running a slim hand through her hair.

His dark brows rose a little. 'If you knew him,' he told her simply, 'you wouldn't cross him,' and Olivia stared at him in silence.

She took a bath later in the afternoon, washing her hair and setting it in the loose, casual style she preferred; her black hair falling around her shoulders in a dark cloud.

As Nick had said he was taking her out to dinner, she decided to do her best *not* to look seductive. Taking out her superbly tailored, rather masculine trouser suit, she smiled to herself. Let him try to make any comment on my figure now! she thought.

The dark blue suit fitted her perfectly, but coupled with a stiff white and blue striped shirt and a blue and red tie done tightly at the neck, it didn't look quite so feminine at all.

Very chic, she told herself with a grin as she looked in the mirror. It had the impact of unleashed sexuality, because of its very masculine appearance in such contrast to her slender curves beneath it. But it wasn't in the least seductive. So Nick couldn't say she was out to get him, which was something to be pleased about.

He arrived back on time, and strolled into the room just as the gilt clock on the mantelpiece struck eight. He looked across at Tonino and raised his dark brows. 'How did it go?'

Tonino gave Olivia a quick, apologetic look, then turned to Nick and nodded briefly.

Olivia flushed hotly as Nick's gaze fell on her. 'So,' he drawled, coming towards her with the tread of a wolf, 'you tried to run away, did you?'

She was angry and she saw no reason to hide it. But although her tone was sharp, she kept her face cool, unwilling to let him see her lose control. 'You knew perfectly well I would,' she pointed out. 'There was no reason to play stupid games.'

Nick studied her for a moment, his body still, the lithe well-muscled contours of it dressed impeccably in the black suit, his white shirt open at the neck. 'Where did you plan to go?' he enquired after a moment, walking towards her. 'To a hotel? Or back to London?' His mouth crooked cynically. 'Or would you like me to guess?'

'Guess away!' she snapped, raising her brows and acting with as much dignity as she could.

'So,' he went over to the drinks cabinet and poured himself a glass of whisky, the amber liquid flowing smoothly into the crystal glass, 'you were going back to

, London.' He replaced the cap and stood the bottle back, closing the cabinet.

Olivia shook her head. 'I'm not that heartless, whatever you might think.' She watched as he walked back to where she stood, one hand holding his glass, the other thrust into the pocket of his trousers. 'I was going to book in at a hotel—just until Greg got better.'

'Really?' he drawled, a sneer in his voice. His hand curled round her wrist and he pulled her to her feet. 'Your compassion for Greg amazes me.' His face hardened. 'It took a hell of a lot to get you here in the first place. What makes you think I'd believe you want to stay?'

Out of the corner of her eye she saw Tonino stand up silently and leave the room, closing the door with a little click. She wished she could do the same.

She looked back at Nick. 'I wish you'd stop blaming me for it,' she said. 'Greg knew I wasn't going to marry him. I gave him no false promises, he knew exactly where he stood right from the start.'

Nick's jaw tightened. 'Which is why, no doubt, you refused to come to see him.' He eyed her, standing directly in front of her, his physical strength making her feel vulnerable as he looked down that arrogant nose at her, the lines of cheek and jaw aggressive. 'I suppose you thought he was just making a dramatic gesture.'

She frowned, considering the question. 'It's possible,' she said slowly, thinking. Greg was a charming young man, but he was quite capable of veering into melodramatics. Although going to these lengths seemed out of character with anyone. She didn't think Greg took himself that seriously, although she could be wrong. 'But that isn't why I didn't want to come,' she said after a pause.

'Oh?' he raised dark brows.

Olivia gave him an irritated look. 'I didn't like your attitude.' He had put her back up from the minute she set eyes on him. Her worry for Greg had been forgotten because of her anger with Nick.

'Which was?' he enquired.

'Arrogant,' she said, easing her wrist from his grasp, her eyes an angry blue as she looked at him. 'You seem to have forgotten how rude you were.' She tilted her head back. 'Or are you normally that insulting?'

His eyes narrowed. 'I thought I was remarkably patient with you, Miss Courtney,' he drawled tightly, and she noticed the way a little muscle jerked in his cheek. 'My brother nearly died because of you. Did you expect me to be pleasant?'

Her brows shot up, and she gave him a sweet smile, holding her anger at being blamed again back. 'Pleasant?' she enquired acidly. 'I doubt if you could be pleasant to anyone.'

His hand snaked out, tangling in her hair as he jerked her towards him. 'Let me tell you something, Miss Courtney,' he muttered, his jaw tight. 'If you hadn't been so damned beautiful, I wouldn't have brought you back at all.'

She tried to pull her head away from him, but his hand tightened further, making her lips part with temper. She stared up at him angrily, aware of the sexual violence that was seeping out of every line of his hard lithe body.

'Do you know,' he drawled, his eyes considering, 'I think I might even want you badly enough to kill, too.' His mouth curled in a cold smile. 'Although I doubt if it would be my own life I'd take.'

'You don't scare me,' she said angrily, her mouth pressed tight in a pale line.

'Don't I?' A flick of his lashes sent his gaze skimming

over her. He raised one dark brow. 'I should.' He watched her for a moment in silence, then ran one long sinewy hand over the dark material of her suit, moving down to her waist. 'Very cool,' he commented sardonically.

She flushed, wishing she hadn't worn the damned thing. 'Let go of me, Mr Baretta, or I'll scream the place down!'

'Scream,' he invited softly. His hand moved to her neck, fingering the tightly buttoned shirt and tie while she stared at him in a hostile silence. 'If that's supposed to put me off, you're in for a shock,' he drawled lazily.

Olivia raised her brows with cold hauteur. 'Don't flatter yourself. I wore this because I like it. Your opinion means very little to me.'

His lips curled in a smile. 'Good. Then you won't object when I tell you how it affects me.'

She couldn't help herself. 'Not at all,' she said in a tight, angry voice.

'It makes me want to rip it off,' he said in a smoky voice.

There was a brief silence as his eyes narrowed on her mouth. She was rigid with anger, her whole body held in a stiff position. 'Let me go!' she clipped out.

Nick laughed under his breath. 'Not a chance.' Her eyes widened as his mouth came down on hers, his lips bruising as he ravaged her with his mouth.

She struggled furiously, punching his chest with balled fists, her arms flailing. He slid his arms round her, holding her tight as he kissed her brutally. She was livid, her face flushing with rage, and she tried to twist her head away from his grasp.

'Keep still,' he muttered, twisting her face back with his hands framing her pale cheeks, the long fingers biting into her flesh as he positioned her head to kiss her again.

Olivia raised her left leg, and brought her stiletto heel

down sharply on his foot.

She heard his painful intake of breath as he released her, and jumped away, her eyes flashing angrily. 'Keep away from me, Mr Baretta!' she warned, picking up the nearest object, 'or I swear I'll hit you with this!'

He stared at her, stunned for a moment. Rage crossed his features for a split second and she held her breath, her heart beating hard against her breastbone.

Then he laughed. 'All right,' he said, shaking his head, 'you've made your point.' He thrust his hands in his pockets, looking down at his feet. The grey eyes flicked back to her with grim humour. 'Although I wish you hadn't made it quite so painfully.'

She relaxed, breathing a sigh of relief. Looking at the object in her hand, she found a heavy brass paperweight. No wonder he decided not to come for me, she thought wryly, replacing it. It would have made a nasty dent in him.

Nick's black head tilted to one side. 'I've booked a table at Lutèce for nine o'clock,' he told her, and raised one dark brow in enquiry. 'Are you ready to leave now?'

She considered him for a moment with a frown, then she nodded slowly. 'Very well.'

'Good.' He smiled and her heart stopped for a second at the charm in his features. 'Give me five minutes to change—they prefer dinner suits.' He walked to his room, closing the door behind him.

Olivia watched him go with a frown. He was a curious man. One minute he had been at her throat, the next he had given her a smile that could have charmed the birds right off the trees. She had to admit, he definitely had his moments.

His reaction to her changed everytime she saw him. What she didn't understand was, why?

CHAPTER THREE

LUTÈCE was the epitome of elegance. They walked in under the blue and white canopy, going down the polished wood steps to the exquisitely furnished restaurant. At the far end was a terrace, and a slight breeze lifted the scent of perfumed blooms through the warm air. Olivia felt a little out of place because it was so obviously exclusive, but refused to show it, meeting the curious gaze of the other women with a cool face. She noticed the covetous glances thrown in Nick's direction as he leaned back in his seat, his body at ease; like a dangerous sexual animal.

Nick eyed her as the first course arrived. 'Very slimming,' he commented drily, looking at the Ogen melon placed in front of her. 'Counting calories?'

Olivia nodded, resting her spoon on the side of the plate. 'My job,' she explained with a slight shrug. 'I have to watch my figure.'

A lazy smile curved his hard mouth. 'So do I,' he drawled, his gaze dropping to her rounded breasts, making her shiver with awareness. 'My compliments,' he said, raising his glass in a toast. 'Your figure is magnetic.'

She flushed and looked away, refusing to rise to the bait. They kept on neutral subjects for the main part of the meal, talking about a range of different things, but underneath the casual words ran an undercurrent of sensuality and danger which she found very disturbing.

'Tell me,' Nick asked suddenly as they ate their dessert, 'why did you choose such a bad moment to drop Greg?'

She sighed heavily and frowned. 'I felt sorry for him because he thought he could make me love him. But he couldn't.' She bit her lip, 'So I went home, and he . . .' she broke off, looking away, unable to finish.

'And he tried to kill himself,' Nick finished for her in an icy drawl. 'Which of course, hadn't occurred to you.'

She looked up sharply, meeting his gaze with narrowed eyes. 'Of course it hadn't!' she said irritably. 'It never entered my head that he would go that far.' Not in a million years would it have occurred to her, in fact, she could still scarcely believe it.

'But he did,' Nick reminded her softly, toying with a knife, the cold blade flashing against the tanned skin of his long fingers. 'What did you think his reaction would be? Or shall I guess?'

Olivia looked away from those sinister features. 'I thought he'd get over it,' she said huskily, 'meet someone else in time.'

'No, Miss Courtney,' he said icily, 'you knew exactly how badly you'd hurt him. I agree, you didn't think he would kill himself. But you knew you'd kicked his teeth in when you left. Playing with men's feelings is a dangerous game.'

'I wasn't playing with his feelings,' she said in a low, angry voice, her hands curling in the crisp white damask tablecloth. 'He knew where he stood all the way down the line.'

There was a little silence. Then Nick asked in a smoky voice, 'Would you like to be hurt, Miss Courtney?' She caught the glint of silver as the knife was pointed casually towards her, the blade flashing under the bright overhead lights.

Her gaze dropped to his hand. 'Are you threatening me?' she asked slowly, her voice unsteady as a frisson of alarm ran down her spine, making her shiver.

Nick's smile was chilling. Then slowly he put the knife back on the table with silent menace.

Her heart thudded a little faster, her pulse beating furiously at her throat. Sitting quite still, she allowed the danger of this man to sink into her. Then she drew a shaky breath and leaned back, not taking her eyes off him.

There had to be some way to get away from him. She could see from his eyes that he wanted to hurt her—she would be a fool not to recognise that predatory, animal look in his eyes. But in Nick it was highly controlled; the threat of sexual violence at once both sinister and wildly exciting, ready to be unleashed at any moment.

But although she knew he wanted to make love to her, she also knew he wanted to hurt her. A dangerous combination, she thought grimly.

They drove home at midnight, and she felt the tension increase at the thought of the coming night. Her pulses leapt with nervous confusion as they entered the apartment side by side, butterflies dancing in her stomach.

'I have to be up early,' Nick told her, walking to her bedroom door with her, 'so I'll say goodnight.'

Olivia was surprised and relieved. 'Oh,' she said, brows rising. 'Okay. Goodnight.'

'You will behave yourself tomorrow, won't you?' he said softly, and one long finger ran down her neck in a deeply sensual movement, making her shiver as the cool fingertip reached the base of her throat where a pulse beat. 'You'll only make me angry if you don't.'

'Of course,' she said huskily, alarmed by her response to the touch of his finger.

'So long as we understand each other,' he drawled lazily. 'I wouldn't want you to get hurt.' He reached out, capturing her chin, tilting her head back till her hair ran in a glossy black cascade. 'Just because I took you out for dinner, it doesn't mean you should start to underestimate me.'

She shivered. There it was again; that sinister threat in his words, even the smoky voice seeming to take on a dangerous note as he spoke. 'I wouldn't dream of underestimating you, Mr Baretta,' she said slowly, keeping her eyes on him, her face wary.

He smiled, and her blood ran cold, her pulses quickening. 'Good,' he murmured, his fingers tightening on her skin, 'because if you did, it could become very dangerous.'

Olivia felt her pulses leap as his black head bent, and his warm mouth fastened on hers in a sensual, coaxing kiss which made her heart thud faster, her mind caught in confusion. His hands slid to her waist, his mouth coaxing hers apart while he drew her against him.

She caught her breath softly as he drew away, staring at him, bewildered, her heart racing.

'Goodnight, Miss Courtney,' he said, 'I expect to see you tomorrow night.' His face held silent menace as he studied her. 'Make sure you're here,' and he turned and walked to his room, leaving her staring after him with a racing heart, her mind in turmoil.

She woke late the next day, surprised to find it was eleven o'clock. She got up and washed quickly, then dressed in a casual outfit of jeans and a silk blouse before going into the living room, yawning a little, still sleepy. To her delight, there was no one around. Her gaze darted around, her ears pricked up as she felt hope rise inside her. If Nick had left her here alone she would have a chance to get away.

The clock ticked on the mantelpiece, softening the silence. A door clicked to her left, and she spun. 'Oh!' she exclaimed, disappointed because Tonino had stayed to keep an eye on her. 'It's you. Where's Mr Baretta?'

Tonino slid his hands into the pockets of a blue-grey double-breasted suit. 'Working,' he told her, his dark face calm. 'Want some breakfast? I been to the deli.'

Olivia shook her head. 'Could I just have coffee?'

'Sure.' Tonino's face was impassive as he walked out of the room, his pace calm and unhurried, his elegant body masculine yet perfectly co-ordinated. She followed him into the bright shiny kitchen and sat on a stool, watching while he poured steaming coffee into a cup and gave it to her.

She observed him as he opened a white paper bag. 'What's that?' she asked, eyeing the freshly baked pastries inside with hunger.

'You want some?' he asked, his face calm. She hesitated, her gaze uncertain, while Tonino watched with dark eyes. 'Is good,' he assured her with total sincerity.

She smiled, her cheeks dimpling. 'Yes, please,' she said, 'I think I'm hungry now.'

'Good!' Tonino's sudden smile gave his face a monkeyish appearance and he busied himself laying out the pastries with elegance and finesse.

They drove to the hospital in the late afternoon. Olivia had made the effort to talk to Tonino about himself, and she felt it was worth it. She knew that making friends with him would be good for her. It was always best to charm the enemy, she thought with a smile.

Greg was delighted to see her. 'Hallo!' he said, sitting up in a bed surrounded with flowers, his eyes recovering a little of their former life. 'All alone today? I suppose Nick's working—he always is.'

She was amazed by the change in him. He was much more lively than he had been, his face still pale and strained, but not as deathly white as yesterday. If that was the effect she had on him, she knew she could not possibly leave him yet.

She sat down on the bed, eyes smiling. 'You look cheerful,' she commented brightly. 'I hope you're going to get even better soon.'

Greg was holding her hand, a little-boy grin on his face. 'Can I have a kiss?' he pleaded, and she felt her heart contract at what she would have to do with him when he was better.

But she gave him a gentle smile, and leaned over. 'Of course,' she said lightly, and dropped a kiss on his nose.

He grimaced. 'Some kiss!' he said, and looked over at Tonino, who stood silently watching. 'Hey, turn your back, Tonino,' he said with a weak laugh, 'I want to kiss my girl!'

Tonino's dark gaze was wise as he looked at Olivia. Then he turned his back silently, sliding his hands into his pockets. He knows, thought Olivia.

'That's better,' said Greg, his hands gentle as he pulled her face down to his and kissed her long and deep. Olivia wanted to cry. He was going to be hurt badly when this was all over. Her lips tightened. It was all Nick Baretta's fault. Some people just didn't know when to leave well alone.

After they had stayed with Greg for two hours, Olivia persuaded Tonino to take her shopping. They drove to Fifth Avenue, and found somewhere to park the car before walking along the shops. Olivia knew her way around, and it was as though she had never left as she looked in familiar shops with Tonino by her side.

'Let's go in here,' she said quickly as she saw a policeman walking around the ground floor of a store.

Tonino shrugged. 'Sure. Why not?' He allowed her to lead him inside and watched with silent amusement as she looked at a rack of dresses.

The store was packed with chattering people, the tills ringing loudly as queues formed and women thrust their purchases at harassed assistants.

Out of the corner of her eye she saw the policeman about to leave. 'I just want to try this on,' she told Tonino, picking up the first dress at hand and hurrying off. 'I won't be a minute.'

'Okay.' Tonino busied himself looking at some silk ties on a rack nearby.

Olivia held her breath, walking in a zigzag around counters to where the policeman stood. 'Officer,' she said quietly, looking over her shoulder, 'can I have a word with you?'

The policeman eyed her with a smile, his face slightly owlish. 'What is it, lady?' he said in a nasal drawl.

'I'm being held against my will in an apartment a few blocks away,' she said in a lowered voice, ignoring his raised brows. 'I want to get away from the people there, but I can't. Can you give me protection?'

The officer frowned. 'Are you serious, lady?' he asked, obviously in doubt as to her sanity. His gaze flicked past her shoulders and a look of recognition crossed his portly features. 'Hallo, Mr Corelli,' he said, and Olivia's heart sank.

Tonino stood calmly next to Olivia. 'Is anything wrong?' he asked in a lilting accent.

'This lady,' the officer indicated Olivia with a little smile, 'says she's being held against her will. Is she with you?'

Tonino's dark eyes flicked slowly to Olivia. 'She's Mr Baretta's guest,' he said, his voice calm. '*Nick* Baretta's guest.'

Olivia felt her heart sink even further as the officer's face changed completely. 'Oh well, in that case,' he tilted his cap and smiled, 'there's no problem. Give my regards to your boss.' He turned and walked away, leaving Olivia to stare after him in helpless anger and frustration.

Tonino took her arm silently, leading her back to put the dress away, then escorting her out of the store. Her lips were tightly compressed as she walked beside him, bitterly angry. She was completely trapped. She wanted to shout and scream with rage, but she walked without a word.

Tonino put her in the car in silence, then walked round calmly to his side, sliding in beside her. He put the keys in the ignition with long slim hands, and started the engine.

He turned his head, his eyes a dark serious brown. 'You shouldn't have done that,' he said quietly. 'Is not going to please him.'

Olivia was tense all night, waiting for him to return. She sat in the living room with Tonino, listening to the endless tick-tock of the gilt clock, her hands moving restlessly on the soft beige armchair while she strained to hear his approaching footsteps. But the suite was silent.

She felt very angry with herself for worrying about his reactions. After all, she had every right to want to leave. He shouldn't be forcing her to stay with him. But even though she was bitterly angry at her own reaction, she couldn't shake off her fear of his return.

'Do you have to tell him?' she asked Tonino hopefully, and Tonino raised his head, putting his paper down.

His eyes held hers. 'What you think?' he asked quietly, and she looked away. He shook his head, looking back at his paper. She picked little threads off the chair arm.

'Do you blame me?' she asked, her voice low and angry.

Tonino sighed. 'Is not the point,' he told her gently. 'The boss—he's going to be very angry.' He looked away and was silent for a moment, then shook his head again and murmured, 'Very angry.'

The door behind them opened, and Olivia's head swung round, her heart leaping with the sudden shock of realising who it must be.

Nick lounged in the doorway wearing a dark waist-coat fitting tightly at the waist, his jacket slung over his shoulder, his long muscular legs drawing the eye encased in the impeccably cut dark trousers.

'Why am I going to be angry, Tonino?' he asked lazily, raising one dark brow.

Tonino glanced at Olivia but didn't say anything.

'Well?' Nick pushed away from the doorjamb, closing the door behind him with a quiet click and walking into the room, sliding one hand into his pocket. The waist-coat emphasised his tight stomach and slim hips.

Tonino stood up, folding his paper and putting it on the table. 'She tried to get away again,' he said quietly.

Nick's lips curled. 'Surprise me!' He flung the jacket on the chair and strolled to the drinks cabinet. 'I've had a hard day,' he said, throwing a glance at Olivia over his shoulder, a brief smile on his lips, 'I need a drink.'

She watched as he opened the cabinet, took out a decanter and crystal glass and poured himself a small measure of whisky. Then he turned lazily, leaning against the cabinet, his long legs stretched before him.

'So,' he drank a little whisky, 'you've been at it again. And I thought you'd learned your lesson.'

She looked at him with intense dislike. 'What lesson?' Her hands curled into fists on the arms of the chair. 'You couldn't teach me how to write my name on a wall!'

He laughed, his lips parting to reveal sharp white teeth. 'I could teach you something a lot more exciting, Miss Courtney,' he drawled, his eyes narrowing on her mouth, and Olivia looked away, her body stiffening with tense dislike.

There was a brief pause, during which Olivia felt the tension increase inside her, as she sat quite still waiting for him to speak again. When he did, she was surprised by what he said, turning her head to look at him wide-eyed.

'I think it's time we had a little discussion,' Nick said flatly, pushing away from the cabinet and walking towards her.

She frowned. 'What about?'

He reached out one hand, the cool fingers encircling her wrist as he pulled her to her feet. 'Coffee for the lady, Tonino,' he said without looking away from her, and Tonino silently stood up and left the room.

Olivia allowed Nick to lead her over to the couch, sitting her down beside him. She watched him closely out of the corner of her eye, wary because he didn't seem as angry as she had expected.

'My brother thinks you're going to marry him,' Nick

told her, and a little smile curled his mouth. 'Somehow, I don't see you doing that—how about you?'

She gave him a sharp, irritated glance. 'I'm not in love with him. Why should I want to marry him?'

He gave her a derisive smile. 'You tell me.'

Olivia felt her temper flare, her head lifting, the light picking out strands of midnight black in her hair. 'Mr Baretta, you're the one who brought me back to Greg. If you'd left well alone, he would have got over me. Instead you've allowed him to believe that I'm back because I love him. If he gets hurt again, it'll be your fault, not mine.'

He ran a comprehensive eye over her, his face brooding. 'I take it that means you're not going to marry him?'

'You take it right.' She met his gaze head on, her face defiant. For a moment she had thought he would try to browbeat her into marrying his brother. But even he wouldn't be that stupid, she realised with relief.

'Which leaves us with the problem of telling him,' he mused, moving so that his arm lay along the back of the couch, almost touching her shoulders. She eyed it with a cool expression.

'He'll have to know,' she agreed, 'sooner or later.'

Nick smiled, and she felt her heart turn over at the charm of his smile. 'I'd prefer later,' he drawled, 'and so would he.'

'I'm not so sure,' she said frowning. Greg had been hurt enough, and she didn't want to be responsible for hurting him even more. But it was unavoidable. She looked back with a sigh. 'I suppose you're right.'

Nick studied her with cool grey eyes. 'You know, I'm beginning to change my ideas about you, Miss

Courtney,' he said in a smoky voice. 'I had you down as a very smart operator with a computer for a heart, but you're making me think I might have been wrong.'

She gave him a sweet, angry smile. 'How generous of you!'

Nick laughed and moved closer to her. 'I'm a very generous man,' he murmured, and his gaze dropped to her mouth. 'When I'm wrong about something, I have the guts to admit it.' His hand slipped to her shoulder, the long fingers caressing her. 'And I could have been wrong about you.'

Olivia felt the searing imprint of his fingers and shivered, avoiding his gaze. 'You were,' she said unsteadily. 'I'm glad you're starting to change your ideas.'

Nick was studying her intensely. 'Oh, I am,' he murmured, his narrowed gaze sharp as he brought one hand up to stroke her cheek. 'You're a remarkably beautiful woman, Olivia,' he added, his voice dropping to a husky murmur.

Her gaze met his with a shock. 'Tonino will be back in a minute,' she said shakily, meeting the full sensual impact of his eyes.

He smiled, his eyes lazy. 'Forget Tonino,' he drawled, pulling her softly towards him. She watched his black head approach with tantalising slowness, her pulse thudding quickly in her throat while her lids closed unconsciously, her head tilting back.

His mouth fastened on hers, warm, coaxing, his kiss deep and soulful, making her pulses leap in confusion as she allowed his long fingers to slide to her shoulders, pushing her gently back against the couch.

Her lips parted and the kiss deepened, her heart racing as she kissed him back, her fingers tangling softly in his thick black hair, while she tried not to think, her mind slightly dizzy.

Nick raised his head, his eyes glittering. 'Yes, I could easily be persuaded into thinking I was wrong about you,' he murmured drily, and Olivia's lids flicked open in disbelief at his words.

Her body slowly iced over as the full meaning of his words sunk in. She stared at him, her face stiff and white. 'You swine!' she breathed through tight lips. 'I'd rather you hated me.'

He laughed, the grey eyes cool. 'Ah, but I do hate you, Miss Courtney,' he drawled. 'That little game you're playing with my brother—you think you can outwit me? I'm no fool. You're destroying him—how could I like a woman capable of that?'

Olivia studied him intensely, her body rigid. 'Why are you doing this?' she asked, totally perplexed. He was deliberately playing some elaborate game with her. She didn't understand why he should go to any trouble just to humiliate her.

Nick smiled, and her blood ran cold. 'I may despise you, but that doesn't make you any the less attractive.' His hand moved to close over her breast. 'I want to fall into your bed, not your heart.'

She tried to slap him then, bitterly angry, her hand flying wildly towards his face. But he was faster, his hand gripping hers before she connected with his cheek, and she stared at him in angry defeat while he smiled down at her.

'I shall have to teach you,' he drawled, 'that every action has a reaction,' and his hands went to her shoulders as he reached for her, trying to pull her back to him.

Olivia pushed him away desperately. 'Touch me again

and I'll have to tell your brother!' she snapped angrily, and her eyes flashed a warning as she held him off with difficulty.

Nick laughed, but his smile was tight, hostile. 'I'm shaking in my shoes,' he drawled, and his black head bent.

'He'd never forgive you!' she flung breathlessly, warding him off with two hands pressed firmly on his hard chest, holding him at arm's length, her face scared and anxious.

Nick raised one dark brow. 'He wouldn't have a choice,' he said with a cold smile, and one long finger ran down her cheek to her mouth, parting her lips sensually. 'Besides, he'd rather I took you before the wedding.'

'I told you,' she said tightly. 'I'm not marrying Greg.'

Nick laughed under his breath, his mouth parting to reveal sharp white teeth. 'So you did,' he drawled. 'Now why is it that I don't believe you?'

Olivia stared at him, her body rigid with incredulous anger. She caught the expression in his eyes, and her breath caught in her throat as she realised what he was saying. Her cheeks ran with hot colour, her anger so vivid she could scarcely move.

'You think I'm after his money,' she breathed, 'don't you?'

Nick eyed her consideringly. 'Mine is a lucrative business, Miss Courtney. Money brings power and power attracts women. I have a great deal of all three. I've learnt to recognise the type—the woman who's after money. I'd be a fool if I didn't see through every hard-hearted little gold-digger that comes along.'

She sucked her breath in, and her hand flew to his cheek with a force that stemmed from incredulous rage.

His head jerked back in surprise, a red stain running along his face as he stared down at her with growing anger. She watched him, her eyes flashing with fury, glad that for one second she had been able to slap that clever smile off his handsome face, make him look at her with more respect than he had before.

He took her shoulders in punitive fingers. 'You never listen, do you?' he bit out, hurting her. 'I warned you— every action has a reaction. And this is mine!'

His hands dragged her towards him and she struggled bitterly, punching him with balled fists while that hard mouth inflicted its punishment on her, pushing her lips back against her teeth until she could stand the pressure no longer.

Trying to twist away, pull her head from his searching ruthless mouth, she writhed beneath him, her breath coming in gasps, but Nick was stronger and his fingers kept her where she was, trapped, unable to escape that angry kiss.

Nick's head lifted, swinging round as the door opened and Tonino came in. 'Get the hell out of here!' he snapped bitingly, his face flushed beneath his tan as he looked at him.

The telephone rang shrilly into the silence as he spoke, and he leaned back with a harsh sigh. 'Answer it,' he told Tonino, who did as he was bid.

Olivia sat up on the couch, breathing fast. She was more thankful than she could say to Tonino. He had come in just at the right moment, and though Nick was obviously still angry, at least he wasn't kissing the living daylights out of her.

Tonino was talking in harsh, rapid Italian. *'Che dite mai? . . . Salvatore è stato uccise?'* His dark head swung to look at Nick sharply.

Nick looked round, his black brows jerking together as he listened intently. Olivia frowned, leaning forwards.

'Dove? . . . Si, noi veniamo.' There was a burst of sound from the earpiece and Tonino raised one slim hand. *'Mi ascolti!'* he said sharply, *'noi veniamo.'* He replaced the receiver, and spun to look at Nick. *'Hai sentito?'*

Nick nodded. 'Yes, I heard.'

Olivia sensed the tension in the room, and looked from one to the other of them, her hair tumbling back in disarray. 'What is it?' she asked, frowning.

Nick looked back at her. 'I have to go out. Something's happened.' He glanced over his shoulder at Tonino. 'Get the car.'

Olivia stood up on shaky legs, following him as he went to the chair, picking up his dark jacket and slipping it on quickly. 'What's happened?' she asked.

'A friend of mine is in trouble,' he told her flatly, and looked at his wrist, the gold watch peeping out from beneath a crisp white cuff, a network of little black hairs on his wrist. 'I don't know how long this will take.'

'Is there anything I can do to help?' she asked as he walked to the door, turning as she finished speaking.

'No.' He shook his head grimly. 'Just stay put.' He opened the door, and looked back at her. 'And Olivia, don't answer the door to anyone. Have you got that? Don't let anyone in—if it's me or Tonino we'll use the key.'

Her eyes widened, until they were a bright startled blue. 'What the hell is going on?' she breathed, staring at him.

Nick hesitated, considering her for a moment. 'I'll explain later,' he told her brusquely. 'Just be here when I get back.' He glanced at Tonino. 'Let's go.'

They left the apartment, and Olivia just stared at the closed door without understanding what on earth had happened. The speed at which things had moved amazed her. A thought occurred to her—would Tonino be coming back to make sure she didn't leave? Quickly, with rising hope, she ran to the window and looked down on the busy streets below.

After a few moments the long black limousine screeched out of the underground garage, its red tail lights disappearing fast into the distance as it joined the snarling traffic. A smile broke on her face and she went to the bedroom.

She dashed round, packing everything, then raced to the door with her case and bag. But when she tried to open the door, she realised with a gasp that it was locked. Incredulity raged on her face for a moment as she struggled with the handle, twisting it, pushing it this way and that before she finally admitted it to herself.

She refused to give up, going to the other doors which led to the corridor outside, trying them all with increasing rage and desperation before she finally slumped against the door with an angry face.

Nick had definitely taken Tonino with him. And neither of them would be back for some time. Which was why they had taken the measures they had to make sure she stayed put.

They had locked her in.

CHAPTER FOUR

SHE stayed up until one in the morning, waiting for their return. In the end, she got sick of waiting, sick of the silent tension which held her still while she listened for their return. She got up slowly and went into her bedroom, getting undressed and getting into bed. She was completely trapped; and she didn't know what to do about it. For a moment she thought of telling Greg what his brother was doing, but she decided against it. Greg wasn't well enough yet to cope with it. Besides, she didn't like the idea of playing off the two brothers against each other.

She slowly began to fall asleep, her tired body relaxing in the softness of the bed. Her lids closed, blocking out all thought, and she started to slip away into sleep.

Sometime in the night, she jerked awake. Listening intently, she heard someone moving about in the next room. She sat up in bed, shaking her head free of sleep, and slipped out of the bed, standing a little unsteadily as she reached for her wrap.

Her bedroom door opened, and Nick stood framed in the doorway, his hand reaching out to flick on the light. He eyed her for a moment, then his hard face relaxed.

He leaned against the doorjamb, his body lazy. 'Exquisite,' he drawled, his gaze skimming over her, tracing the silhouette of her naked body beneath the flimsy nightgown. 'Is this my welcoming party?'

Olivia slipped her wrap on, jerking it together at the waist, her eyes closing a little at the glare of the light. 'I'd rather welcome a scorpion!' she snapped, her face angry.

Nick laughed, his mouth parting to reveal sharp predatory white teeth. 'I've already told you,' he drawled, his eyes on her rounded breasts, 'I'm deadlier than any animal you could come up with. And I sting faster than any scorpion.'

Olivia compressed her mouth, pulling the soft wrap closer to herself at the neck, trying to disguise the pale skin of her breasts. 'You locked me in,' she said angrily. 'Why?'

He raised one dark brow, folding his arms in a leisurely way. 'Now why do you think?'

She flushed, feeling foolish. 'There was no need to do it,' she said, keeping her cool. 'You would have come and got me back even if I had got away. So what would be the point in my making a bid for freedom?'

He smiled, and her blood chilled. 'You're beginning to understand me, Miss Courtney. Let's keep it that way, shall we?'

He studied her for a moment in silence, then pushed away from the doorjamb, coming towards her slowly. 'Were you asleep?' he asked, stopping in front of her.

Her brows rose in surprise. 'Yes,' she said, eyeing him warily. 'Why do you ask?'

'My compliments, once again,' he said, his voice dark and sexy, his eyes tracing her soft face, without make-up, the way her soft hair fell about her shoulders in natural waves. 'I can't wait to see your lovely face on my pillow when I wake up.'

Olivia stiffened angrily. 'You'll just have to bear the

suspense,' she said tightly, flushing at the look in his eyes.

He laughed. 'The excitement of the chase always sharpens my interest,' he drawled, and his eyes glittered with intense sensuality. 'It adds a little spice, don't you agree?'

Olivia felt the colour rise in her cheeks, and looked away, flustered and angry. 'Why did you go out?' she asked, trying to steer away from that particular subject. 'What had happened?'

Nick shrugged. 'Some people broke into my offices. I thought one of the men on duty had been killed, but his injuries weren't fatal.' He looked back at her and raised one dark brow. 'Satisfied?'

Olivia nodded, trying to appear nonchalant. 'I'm rather tired,' she said slowly, 'I think I'll go back to bed. Goodnight.' She eyed him in the hope that he'd go away.

His mouth crooked sardonically. 'Running scared, Miss Courtney?' he drawled, and turned to walk out of the room. 'Goodnight,' he said with a dry smile.

Olivia breathed a sigh of relief. For one moment she had thought he might try to seduce her. What worried her most was whether she would have been able to resist that firm mouth, those experienced hands.

He was dead right: he had her running scared. The sooner she got away from him the better. Her mind was spinning as she got back into bed, resting her head on the pillow. The only thing she could do was wait until Greg got better, then get as far and as fast away from Nick as possible.

She spent the next few days visiting Greg in hospital.

Nick was rarely at the apartment, and when he was they spoke to each other over an undercurrent of tension that sapped at her strength, made her pulse go haywire every time he was near. She would look up to find him watching her with narrowed, intent eyes, and she would feel a shiver of awareness run through her.

When she saw Greg, he talked to her about their marriage, and she sat holding his hand and wanting to kill Nick Baretta for forcing her into such an agonising position. When she saw Nick she felt a mixture of emotions run through her as she responded to his intense sexuality, as well as to his antagonism.

One afternoon, later in the week, she managed to ring Alistair. He answered, sounding harassed as usual.

'Olivia!' Alistair could be pictured bouncing around agitatedly, his curly red hair matching his face. He was a man who went through life like a steam train out of control, blowing his whistle to warn everyone else to jump out of his way as he tore down the tracks at high speed, steam coming out of his ears. 'Where have you been? I haven't heard from you for a week!'

She smiled, her full mouth curving. 'I've been a bit tied up,' she said drily, tongue in cheek. Her mind flashed a visual image of Nick and her face tightened.

'Well, you should have rung earlier,' Alistair grunted, and she imagined him rapping his bony fingers impatiently on his desk. 'Imagine leaving me to cope with this lot on my own!'

She frowned, detecting a note of real worry in his voice. 'Cope with what on your own?' she asked slowly.

'No point in beating around the bush,' he said bitterly. 'We've been losing money hand over fist. The whole place is crashing down around our ears.'

Olivia drew her breath in, sitting up straight. 'Alistair!' she exclaimed, alarmed and incredulous, 'why didn't you tell me?'

'Well,' he retorted irritably, 'you didn't ask, did you? I thought your deal with Montoux might pull us out of the mud, but they put the word out after you pushed off, and half the girls have been unable to get work since.'

Olivia's hand tightened on the receiver as she thought of Nick's selfish behaviour in bringing her here. 'Isn't there anything you can do?' she asked.

'I wish there was,' he said grimly, 'but it's too late. We've been having talks with some big mega-star company who wants to buy us up. The deal is almost clinched.'

Olivia rested her cheek in the palm of her hand, sighing with exasperation. She was going to be handed over to some other company, and it was all Nick's fault for interfering.

'So you're definitely selling out,' she stated, closing her eyes with defeat.

'No choice, dear,' Alistair said bitterly. 'These big shots have got the money we need to inject some blood into our bank balance. But don't worry, I'll still be working here.'

She nodded, seeing her entire world slip away out of her hands. 'I'm sorry,' she said, closing her eyes again, 'I didn't realise things were so bad.'

Alistair hesitated for a moment, then sighed. 'Forget it. I'm sure I'll enjoy working under the mega-stars. Maybe they'll teach me some new tricks of the trade.'

Poor Alistair, Olivia thought grimly. Now someone would be controlling him, and all his restless energy would be channelled, taking away half his life blood in the process. The train would have to slow down, and Alistair would become bitter.

She talked to him for a few more minutes, trying to keep the conversation lively. She avoided all questions about Nick Baretta, unwilling to discuss him more than necessary. She was too angry to think about the man; he had destroyed her agency, and probably her career.

She spent the day with Tonino as usual, going to the hospital, doing a little shopping, trying to keep things on the same easy, friendly basis that they had slipped into. When they arrived back, Tonino unpacked his shopping with a bright grin.

'I make you the best meal you ever had,' he told her, ushering her out of his kitchen. 'Is big surprise, so you stay there and wait.'

She went obediently into the living room, and read a magazine she had bought in town. After about three-quarters of an hour, the door burst open and he re-appeared, grinning like mad. He had made her a huge bowlful of beautifully cooked spaghetti bolognese which he produced with a flourish, like a conjuror bringing his rabbit out of the hat.

'Delicious!' Olivia said with a brave smile, beginning to eat.

'No!' Tonino was horrified, watching with amazement. 'Not like that—I show you.'

He took her spoon and fork and gave her a calm lesson on how to curl the long pale strands around her fork, his slim hands demonstrating with great elegance.

She did her best to copy his effortless style, and succeeded a little, smiling at him as she ate. Tonino nodded with approval and sipped a little of the Lambrusco he had served with the meal.

'My girl,' he told her with a smile, 'she cooks the best spaghetti in the whole of Sicily.' He grinned, his face lighting up mischievously. 'That's why I'm going to marry her.'

Olivia smiled, then a thought occurred to her. 'Are you Sicilian, Tonino?' She tilted her head to one side. 'I thought you were Italian, like Nick.'

Tonino frowned, his dark face serious. 'Italian? Nick's family are from Sicily. Didn't you know?'

No, she didn't know. She had never thought to ask either Nick or Greg. Their names and friends suggested Italian descent—it had never occurred to her that they might be Sicilian. She had just accepted the fact that they were New Yorkers by birth, with Italian connections. She had never met anyone from Sicily before.

She looked at Tonino with a little smile. 'Sicily . . .' she said considicringly. 'Isn't that where the Mafia come from?'

Tonino laughed with delight. 'No,' he told her, grinning, his thin mouth parting to show little white teeth, 'they go over to Naples, kill everybody, then come home to Sicily to pray.'

She stared at him, shocked. 'What?'

Tonino pursed his lips. 'Is terrible, I know. But,' he shrugged philosophically, 'is life.' He looked across at her stricken face. 'Eat, eat, eat!' he told her, grinning. 'Is my little joke!'

Slowly she began to eat, her eyes wide as she continued to stare at him. She got the feeling it was not his little joke, but she decided not to bring the subject up again. It was best not to talk about things like that.

Nick came in after they had finished eating and were

drinking their coffee. He walked into the room, rubbing one hand over the back of his neck, eyeing them with a tired face.

'God, I'm exhausted,' he muttered, giving Tonino a brief smile. 'Any coffee left?'

Tonino looked up. 'Sure, boss.' He gestured towards the china coffee pot on the table. 'Plenty—in there.'

Nick strolled lazily into the kitchen and came back with a cup, pouring himself some coffee and sitting down in an armchair, his long legs stretched before him as he relaxed, sighing. He lifted the cup to his lips and drank, closing his eyes briefly.

'How's Greg?' he asked suddenly, looking across at Olivia.

She returned his gaze calmly. 'Much better. Haven't you been to see him?' She raised one brow, still angry with him for keeping her here. 'I thought you were the one who was losing sleep over him.'

His eyes narrowed. 'I saw him this morning,' he said brusquely. 'I wanted to know how you were getting on with him.'

Olivia flushed, feeling foolish. She hadn't meant to sound spiteful, she had just wanted to make him feel bad for trapping her. She frowned, sipping her coffee in silence. Alistair's words came back to her and she raised her head, frowning as she looked across at Nick, her head tilted to one side.

'When do you think I can go home?' she asked, angry with herself for phrasing it that way, but not wishing to start an argument with him for no reason.

He raised his black head. 'I haven't decided yet.'

Olivia felt her mouth compress with irritation. 'You can't keep me here for ever,' she pointed out. 'I have a family in London, and a job to get back to.'

'Ah yes,' he drawled with a sneer, 'your job.'

Her lips tightened. 'I've told you before—I have to earn a living somehow, and sitting around in New York isn't going to pay my rent.'

Nick stood up, his dark face brooding. He walked over to the window and leaned against the wall, his back to her, without replying. She watched him with a growing anger, annoyed at the casual way he treated her and her life, pushing her around without a thought to what she would have to face on returning to London.

'I'll pay your rent,' he told her coldly, without looking at her. 'Tell me when it's due and I'll send a cheque to whoever's concerned.'

She put her cup down with a little clatter. 'I don't want you to pay my rent,' she snapped through pale lips, 'I want to go home and get back to work!'

He turned his head, his eyes angry. 'Why the hell is your job so important to you?' he asked. 'All you do is stand around half-naked all day while some leering idiot takes pictures of you.'

Olivia sucked her breath in, glaring at him with hatred. 'That isn't true!' she protested between her teeth, amazed at the insult, her eyes wide, sparkling a bright angry blue against the vulnerable curve of her pale cheek.

Nick laughed coldly. 'Oh no, of course it isn't.' He watched her over his shoulder with cold grey eyes. 'Then what was that deal you signed with Montoux? They sell lingerie, as far as I know.'

Olivia flushed, her cheeks holding a bright red coin of anger. 'I was going to model nightclothes,' she told him tightly, trying to keep her temper in check. It was true—

she hadn't signed to model underwear, some other girl had been asked to do that.

'Which isn't the same thing, of course,' he drawled icily, pushing away from the window and walking towards her, his hands thrust into the pockets of his trousers.

'No,' she said tight-lipped, 'it's not.'

He studied her for a moment, his eyes angry. 'That charming nightdress you were wearing the other night,' he said, his gaze sweeping over her, 'that was a Montoux number, wasn't it?'

Olivia flushed hotly, remembering the night he had come to her room and seen her in it. It was a pale blue long shift, which was almost completely see-through with sea-green straps and a bodice which showed her rounded breasts seductively, the gown falling in a straight line to her feet, her silhouette visible beneath it.

'They gave me some as part of the deal,' she muttered, looking away from those knowing eyes.

Nick laughed. 'I'm sure they did,' he drawled, and his mouth parted to reveal predatory white teeth. 'What else did they give you?'

She jerked her head back, her face bitterly angry. 'A contract,' she snapped, 'nothing else.'

Nick held her gaze for a moment in silence, and their eyes warred briefly. Then she shrugged, dropping the subject. 'All the same, the work you do is hardly important. The world won't fall apart without you, Miss Courtney. There's no hurry for you to get back.'

She stared at him in hostile silence, feeling her temper rise like a wild flame inside her. 'How dare you do this to me!' she snapped in a low, angry voice. 'You can't run my life for me. I'm a human being, not a piece of paper on a file in your office!'

He looked at her, and she backed from the flare that leapt in his grey eyes. 'A piece of paper is the last thing I would have compared you with,' he said thickly. 'You're much more shapely than that.'

Olivia gritted her teeth, ignoring the deliberate reference to her body. 'My agency is in trouble,' she said, standing up to face him, her fists clenching at her sides. 'I have to go back or they'll fall apart.'

Nick watched her consideringly, then one dark brow rose. 'You've been in touch with them, have you?'

She nodded, controlling her laboured breathing. She was so angry she thought the top of her head might blow off and she'd erupt all over the room like a sizzling firecracker.

'And what did they say?' Nick drawled, one hand reaching inside his jacket pocket. He took out a cigar and lit it, the silver-blue tendrils of smoke weaving in a silent ribbon around his dark face, his eyes narrowed a little against the smoke.

She watched the lighter flick shut, and the glint of gold as he put it back in his pocket. 'They're in financial trouble,' she told him. 'The deal I had with Montoux would have pulled them back into the black, but because you made me cancel it, they've sunk deeper into the red.'

He nodded, drawing on the cigar, tapping a little ash into a silver ashtray on the table. 'Are you asking me for help, Miss Courtney?' he asked sardonically.

She drew in her breath furiously. 'I wouldn't ask you for a bent farthing!'

Nick's mouth indented. 'How noble of you,' he drawled cynically. 'But it's too late, I'm afraid.'

She watched him, standing totally still in a little silence that followed. Then she said slowly, 'What do you mean?'

He drew on his cigar, the smoke curling around his black head. 'I bought your agency up this morning. The deal was finalised at eleven-thirty a.m.'

She stared at him, her mind whirling. Why had he bought her agency? It wasn't a big place, it didn't do a lot of business. Alistair just handled a few select models—not top models, but pretty successful ones. It wasn't exactly a going concern in the way that it made millions—which made it all the more astounding that Nick Baretta should want to buy them out.

'Your contract,' he continued, 'came part and parcel with the rest of the outfit.' His grey eyes flicked over her slowly, the black lashes resting on his tanned cheek. 'I own you, Miss Courtney—lock, stock and barrel.'

Fury raged inside her as she stared at him, her face running through the whole gamut of emotions, as though her mind was on display, and Nick Baretta read every emotion on her face with amusement. She wanted to hit him, to knock that sardonic smile off his face. She kept her hands tightly by her side, afraid to move in case she provoked his temper.

'Why?' she asked through tightly clenched lips.

He shrugged. 'A little whim of mine.' He gave her a chilling smile. 'I like to make sure I have control over things. That way, nothing gets away from me.'

Bitter anger flared in her eyes. 'You'll never have control over me!'

He took a step closer to stand directly in front of her. 'Won't I?' he drawled sardonically, and his eyes traced her face. 'I wouldn't be too sure about that, Olivia.'

She felt a pulse begin to beat in her throat at the look

in his eyes. The way he spoke her first name in that caressing, smoky voice made a shiver run through her.

'You can't pull my strings, Mr Baretta,' she said unsteadily, her heart skipping a beat at the expression on his brooding face. 'I'll cut my losses and go elsewhere.'

'And I'll follow.' His hand snaked out, capturing her chin and tilting her head back, his forefinger and thumb caressing her skin.

She stared into his eyes with growing alarm. 'Let go of me,' she said through dry lips.

He smiled, making her heart turn over, and his head came closer until his mouth fastened on hers in a warm, coaxing sensual kiss, making her head spin dizzily as she tried to resist the growing need to kiss him back, yield in his arms.

He raised his head. 'You see?' he said mockingly, and Olivia stared at him in a dumb silence.

She stepped back, unable to hold his gaze, and turned to walk stiffly into her room. She heard his mocking laughter behind her as she walked, and tried to ignore it, the husky sound caressing her nerve-ends.

'Miss Courtney,' he drawled as she opened her door.

She turned, her face tightly controlled. 'Yes?'

Nick studied her broodingly. 'I have the day off tomorrow. We'll go to see Greg in the afternoon.'

Olivia nodded stiffly, then closed her door behind her, locking it and leaning against the wooden panels with a growing sense of despair.

Nick wanted her very much, but he also wanted to hurt her. He wouldn't forgive her for hurting Greg, he had made that clear, but he was also determined, as far as she could see, to make her want him, or rather admit she wanted him.

She sighed, her frown marring her brow as she sank on to her bed. She hadn't guessed at how strong her attraction to him was. Every time he looked at her in a certain way, she felt herself responding to the flare in his eyes, felt herself shiver every time he touched her.

She had to make him think she wasn't interested. But how? Grimly she pushed the thoughts away from her mind and took out a magazine she had bought earlier, trying to read it as she sat awake in bed. But her mind was too full, too alive with thoughts. The words blurred in front of her, and she put it down with a sigh, her eyes stinging with hot tears. There just didn't seem to be a way out.

Just before they left for the hospital, there was a phone call. Tonino went calmly across the room to answer it, his double-breasted suit heightening his elegance, his sense of style. He deftly picked up the receiver.

A smile lit his face, and he began talking in rapid Italian. After a moment, he put one hand over the mouthpiece and turned his head to look over at Nick.

'Is Simonetta,' he told Nick. 'She wants to know when she can see Greg.'

Nick's eyes met Olivia's. 'Soon,' he murmured, and his mouth curved in a slow, lazy smile that made her eyes narrow suspiciously, her body tensing as she looked at him.

They drove to the hospital in silence. Olivia sat in the car beside Nick, looking at him from time to time, wondering who Simonetta was, wondering why his smile had made her uneasy.

Whenever she looked round, she met his gaze, and

was startled by the intensity in it. She looked quickly away, unable to hold it for longer than a few seconds.

Greg was cheerful but restless. 'When can I get out of this place?' he asked as they sat in the hospital with him, Olivia on his right, Nick on his left.

Olivia was pleased and relieved by his quick recovery. 'I hope you can leave soon,' she said, placing her hand over his with a smile. 'The sooner the better.' Her eyes met Nick's over the bed.

Greg smiled tenderly. 'Missing me?'

'Of course.' She gave him a gentle smile, but looked away, patting his hand guiltily.

Greg watched her for a moment with a contented smile, then turned to Nick. 'Hey, you can be our best man!' he said with a bright grin. 'I've always seen you in top hat and tails!'

Nick's eyes flicked to Olivia. 'Planning a Victorian wedding, are you?' he drawled.

Greg grimaced. 'Yes, I know,' he said sighing, 'Mamma won't like it, but she'll just have to lump it. After all,' he shrugged, 'I've lived in the States all my life—I'm more American than Sicilian.'

Olivia listened grimly, her face paling as she thought of the bitter disappointment Greg would have when he found out she wasn't going to marry him. She looked involuntarily at Nick, her eyes cold, blaming him for all this, wishing he would stop running her life. He was going to hurt Greg again with his obstinacy.

Greg turned to her with a grin. 'You haven't met Mamma yet, have you? She's a formidable lady— brought us up single-handed. It must have been tough on her, all alone in a strange city like this.'

Nick gave his brother a brief smile. 'She'll meet her

soon,' he told him, glancing at Olivia, and she thought she detected a slight hardening of his features as the talk of weddings continued.

Greg turned to Olivia, his grin mischievous. 'Have you bought your wedding dress yet? I hope it's sexy! I want to show you off to all my friends.'

She drew a ragged breath. 'Let's not talk about it any more,' she said huskily, 'it's bad luck.'

She couldn't bear it. He was storing up trouble for himself and there was nothing she could do to stop him. All she could do was hope that he would be recovered by the time he found out the truth.

'I've spoken to Dr Leslie,' said Nick, leaning back lazily, 'and he says you'll be ready to leave in a couple of days.'

Greg's face broke into delighted surprise. 'Great!' he exclaimed. 'Why didn't you tell me before?'

Nick's mouth crooked sardonically. 'I wanted it to be a surprise,' he drawled, a flick of his lashes sending his gaze skimming to Olivia, who watched suspiciously, her face wary.

'Isn't that wonderful?' Greg pressed her hand happily.

'Wonderful,' she agreed, her eyes kind. The time was swiftly approaching for her to tell him the truth, and she didn't think she would be able to hurt him when the time came.

'I've decided to take you away to convalesce,' Nick announced.

Olivia looked at him sharply, suddenly filled with unaccountable alarm. Unease stirred inside her as she looked at Nick, and her heart began to beat in a slow heavy rhythm.

'Where to?' Greg asked eagerly, almost leaping out of the bed with enthusiasm. 'Somewhere hot, I hope. I could do with some sunshine after this place. It's like living in Dracula's castle!'

Nick's face took on a calculating, sinister appearance. 'I'm taking you home,' he told him smokily, and his gaze flicked to Olivia's. 'To Solunto.'

'Solunto?' she ventured, leaning forward, her throat tight as her gaze was riveted on Nick.

A slow, lazy smile curved his mouth. 'Sicily,' he said softly, and she felt her heart stop.

Sicily! Olivia's stricken face conveyed her feelings as she felt her body freeze. If he took Greg to Sicily, would he expect her to come along too? She wouldn't go. There was no way. But on the other hand, he might have decided to get Greg as far away from her as possible.

That must be it, she thought bitterly. Nick wanted her out of the picture, right out of it. He didn't want her anywhere near Greg. Well, that suited her fine. She was very fond of Greg, she cared for him, but she was not marrying him to please his brother.

She relaxed, and came back down to earth, listening as Greg and Nick talked to each other. She felt relieved that her brief sojourn with Nick in his apartment was over.

'I can't wait,' Greg said with little-boy excitement. 'Can you, Olivia?'

She looked down at him with an absent smile, then his words sank in and her eyes narrowed. She frowned. 'Can't wait?' she repeated, trying not to show her alarm.

He raised his brows in surprise, then ruffled her hair with one lazy hand. 'You're getting worse,' he said with tenderness, his eyes affectionate as he looked up at her. 'You haven't been listening. Tell her, Nick,' he said with a smile.

Her eyes slowly met Nick's. 'We're going to stay in the family's home in Sicily,' Nick drawled, and his mouth indented with cynical amusement. 'All three of us.'

Olivia stared at him, her eyes wide as she took it in. Then her temper began to rise inside her as she saw the mocking smile curl his firm mouth. She wanted to slap the smile off his face.

'We could get married there,' Greg mused.

But Olivia wasn't listening. She was staring at Nick Baretta with intense hatred.

CHAPTER FIVE

'I AM not going, and that's final!' Olivia ground out between tightly clenched teeth as she faced Nick Baretta across the living room of his apartment.

The journey back from the hospital had been nerve-racking; the snarling noise of the traffic had grated on her nerves, edging her tension higher, pummelling her until she felt her nerves seize up like tightly coiled wire, her mouth compressing in an angry line. They had argued constantly; Olivia with increasing desperation, Nick with a biting drawl which both scared and alarmed her.

'I don't want him to have a relapse,' Nick said now, standing by the window, and his black head swung to look at her as he spoke. 'Sicily is the perfect place for him at the moment.'

'But not for me,' she snapped, her eyes flashing angry blue sparks. There was no way she was going. No way.

'Use your head,' Nick drawled tightly. 'If you don't go with him he'll know you're not going to marry him. Do you want to be responsible for what he might do when he finds out?'

Tears of frustrated rage stung her eyes, but she refused to let them show, refused to give up. 'He's a grown man!' she protested. 'He's old enough to take it.'

'But he's not.' He watched her with narrowed, intense eyes, then came towards her swiftly, his hard-boned face without expression. 'He's already proved that. He's weak. He can't handle his own emotions. This time he might really kill himself.'

'Is that my fault?' Olivia demanded, her hands clenching into fists at her sides as she struggled to keep a hold on her temper. She knew she was getting nowhere fast.

Nick's black head tilted to one side, his eyes angry. 'Don't you ever learn?' he asked. 'You pushed him to the brink once before and watched him topple over— are you trying to do it again?'

She drew a shaky breath. 'I didn't do it deliberately and you know it!' she said, her voice husky with guilt, her eyes a vivid blue against the pale curve of her cheek.

'I hope not,' Nick drawled icily, a flick of his lashes sending his gaze skimming over her, his own features menacing, sinister, 'because if I ever find out that you did . . .' his hand caught her hair roughly, jerking her towards him, 'I'll kill you.'

She shivered, alarm running through her as she stared at him in silence for a second. She caught her breath with fear and excitement as he stepped closer, his hand tangling tighter in her hair.

'You're coming to Sicily, Miss Courtney,' he told her smokily, 'if I have to drag you every step of the way myself. And don't think for one second that I wouldn't.'

Her eyes were wide, holding bitter contempt. 'You're capable of anything,' she said through pale lips, her hands clenched into fists at her sides.

Nick's mouth curled. 'You'd better believe it,' he drawled, his voice a smoky threat. He watched her for a moment with narrowed steely eyes, making sure the threat sank home. Then he released her with a jerk and turned to walk to the table, flipping open the polished wood cigar box, taking out a cigar and clamping it between his teeth.

'For God's sake!' Olivia protested, taking one last chance, 'can't you see how unfair you're being? I have a life of my own—friends, a family, a job to get back to.'

His black head turned with chilling slowness. 'My brother,' he said bitingly between tightly clamped teeth, 'is in hospital with bandages over his wrists, and you tell me I'm unfair?'

She flushed hotly, her hands twisting together in angry confusion, guilt and frustration written on her face. 'You're being selfish!' she flung, her eyes darting wildly, her breathing fast. 'You're only seeing it from one point of view . . .'

'*Enough!*' Nick's hand crashed on the table and he spun, coming towards her, temper evident in every line of that dangerous, ruthless face, his eyes leaping with anger.

Olivia jumped, backing away, seeing the menace, the threat of violence in his body. Her heart leapt in her breast, her pulses skidding.

Nick stood in front of her, iron self-control evident on his face. His hands gripped her shoulder, the long fingers punitive. 'Now,' he drawled tautly, 'one more word out of you, just one more word, and you'll find yourself in trouble. Do I make myself clear?'

She stared at him, their eyes warring for a second. Then she nodded, her mouth compressing with bitterness.

He smiled, and her blood ran cold. 'Good,' he murmured, and spoke to Tonino without taking his eyes off her. 'Nino, keep an eye on her. Don't let her out of your sight.'

Tonino came to stand next to Olivia, looking down at her angry face with dark unreadable eyes. 'Sure, boss,' he said quietly, and Olivia eyed him with barely concealed resentment.

'She's as cunning as a fox,' Nick told him as he turned to walk towards the door. 'Don't trust her an inch.' His gaze flicked to Olivia with a cool smile, then he turned on his heel and left the flat, leaving her and Tonino to stare after him in silence.

Tears of rage spurted from her eyes and her hands flew to her face as they flowed unchecked down her cheeks. She was bitterly angry, scared and filled with burning resentment.

Tonino watched as she sank on to the couch, crying, then he left the room quietly, coming back with a large box of tissues which he handed to her. She took one of the bright-coloured soft pieces and wiped her eyes with a trembling hand. Tonino sat down next to her, his eyes sympathetic.

Looking up at him, she said, 'You must see how unfair it is?' Her eyes searched his for a flicker of understanding, but on his wise dark face she saw only sympathy. 'Tonino,' she said urgently, 'can't you help me? Let me get away while he's out?'

Tonino raised his dark brows. 'You crazy?' he asked, observing her down his hooked nose. 'He'd have me shot!'

Olivia sighed, feeling helpless, frustrated at every turn. There had to be a way out. Tonino couldn't help her. She was out on her own with this one. Nick Baretta had her right under his thumb, and he wasn't going to let her wriggle out of his grasp.

She was in a state of deep nervous tension for the rest of the day. She bit her nails incessantly, right down to the quick, her mouth moving in obsessive jerky movements until the back of her neck felt like an iron clamp, her head throbbing with stress.

Tonino sat with her, his dark face sympathetic as he watched her, but he said nothing, and she looked away from him, trying to think of some way out.

At midnight, Tonino put his book down and came over to where she sat. 'Get some rest,' he told her gently. 'Is no good for you staying up all the time.'

She looked up, her eyes bitter. 'What's the point? I wouldn't be able to sleep even if I tried.'

Tonino eyed her for a moment in silence. Then he disappeared from the room, leaving her with a slight frown. Olivia shrugged. What did she care where he had gone? She went back to her restless thoughts, her mouth tightly closed.

'Here,' Tonino came back with a glass of water and two round white pills. He handed them to her. 'To help you sleep,' he explained as she stared at them.

Panic rose inside her as she lifted the glass to her lips. Why should he want to give her sleeping pills? She kept them in her palm, pretending to swallow them as she sipped at the glass of water and handed it back to him with an obedient smile.

'Good girl,' Tonino nodded with approval, as he took the glass back. 'Now, you go to sleep. Is very late.'

Olivia stood up, acting casually, and slipped the pills into the pocket of her dress. Tonino hadn't noticed a thing. As far as he was concerned, she had taken the pills and was about to fall into a very deep sleep.

She went into her room, saying goodnight, and gave

a sigh of relief as she closed her door behind her. She got undressed and slipped into bed, lying awake for long tense minutes, her mind whirling in circles as she explored every avenue she could think of. She always met with the same unscalable brick wall blocking her escape.

An idea hit her, and getting out of bed, she slipped her wrap on, putting the sleeping pills into the pocket and tiptoeing to her door. Tonino was still up—she could hear him moving around outside. She bit her lip, praying that her idea would work, and opened the door.

Tonino looked up with a frown. 'What is it?' he asked, putting his whisky down on the table with a clink and getting up.

Olivia forced a casual smile. 'I'm thirsty,' she said, her eyes dropping to the whisky glass by his side. She looked up again. 'I thought I'd get some water.'

His face relaxed into an understanding smile. 'Sure. Is the pills—they make you thirsty.' He nodded to a chair, his eyes sympathetic. 'You stay here. I get you some water.'

Olivia was tense as she returned his smile. As soon as he had left the room, she went to the table where his whisky stood. Fixing her eyes on the door and straining her ears, she fumbled inside her pocket for the pills and took them out quickly.

They were a little soggy, but they would dissolve easier that way. With trembling hands, she put them in the whisky. Her heart skipped a beat—they weren't dissolving!

Desperately she stirred them with her forefinger. Then she reached for the soda syphon. Her hand slipped and the spray went on herself. She cursed under her breath.

Tonino's footsteps approached the door and she closed her eyes, praying for time. The soda squirted with a hiss into the glass, disguising the white foam.

'What are you doing?' Tonino's voice made her jump, splashing soda off the side of the glass in panic.

'I . . .' her hands shook as she put the heavy glass syphon down, 'I thought you might like a little soda.' She shrugged, her throat dry. 'I wouldn't want you to get drunk.'

Tonino's thin lips drew back into a little smile. 'Is okay. I'm going to bed now.' He handed her the glass of water and grinned. 'I take my whisky and a good book. Is better than sleeping pills!'

Olivia tried to control her trembling hands as she took the water and went back to bed. The breath was forced out of her in intense relief as she closed the door behind her and leaned against it, her eyes shut tight, her body relaxing slowly.

Ten minutes later, she was dressed and packed. The lift took her swiftly down to the ground floor. She held her breath, frightened that she would bump into Nick on his way back to the apartment, but there was no sign of him.

She was in the street sixty seconds later. The night air hit her like a blast of shock treatment and she dodged into the shadows, more afraid of Nick's possible return than of the night-people who lurked in the city streets, their shadows waiting for her.

The raw pulsing energy of New York injected courage into her. She turned the block, walking faster, looking over her shoulder quickly, her eyes darting around. Night-people walked past her, strolling, eyeing her curiously. The traffic snarled along the road, horns blasting, brakes squealing, red tail lights blazing, while bright headlights blinded her.

Her heart leapt furiously as she spotted a cab, and jumping into the road, she hailed it. 'Kennedy Airport, please,' she gasped out, slamming the metal door harshly, 'as fast as you can!'

The driver's voice came through the wire mesh screen. 'Okay, lady,' he said, his foot pressing the gas pedal. 'Watch my dust!' and they pulled away quickly.

She hid behind her hands as they drove past Nick's apartment. It wasn't until they were well clear of the area that Olivia felt herself begin to relax. Her heart lifted with sheer incredulity. She was free! She leaned back in the taxi, her eyes closed with lighthearted relief, her hands resting on the edges of the knife-scarred leather seats. The inside of the taxi made her smile— graffiti covered every spare inch of it, most of it scratched in with a penknife.

They drove down the stylish East Side until they came to the East River. Olivia gazed out with wonder as they drove past, seeing the lights dancing on the surface of the night-blackened water, shining and leaping where the water dappled. Then there were underpasses, overpasses and dirty streets which reminded her of London's East End, only worse.

The freeway to the airport reminded her of the drive into Kent. Great banks rose up from either side, with bungalows and houses dotted along the top. Headlights blinded as the drivers on the opposite lanes zoomed past into New York.

Thirty-five minutes later she stepped out at Kennedy Airport. She went straight over to the British Airways desk, booked her flight, used almost all of her credit rating on the ticket and went over to the café, telling herself it was money well spent.

The clock ticked endlessly by, and she felt fatigue tighten her muscles as she waited for her flight to be called. When it was, she walked swiftly to Passport Control, making her way to the yellow light through the crowds.

'Going somewhere?' A drawling voice made her heart leap with fear, and she spun, her eyes widening. Nick caught her arm as she tried to get away. 'Not so fast!' he said tightly, pulling her back against him, forcing the breath out of her as she landed hard against his chest.

'How did you know I was here?' she asked angrily, staring at him in frustration.

A cold smile curved his lips. 'I drew the obvious conclusions when I got home to find Tonino out like a light.' He raised one brow, his expression icy. 'You're quite a lethal lady. Whatever it was you slipped in his drink knocked him out stone cold.'

Olivia looked away, clenching her fists. 'So what happens now?' Her voice was low, angry. 'I'm not coming back now that I've got this far. I want to go home—you can't stop me!' There were too many people around. He wouldn't dare to force her out of here under all these watchful eyes.

He smiled, and her blood ran cold. 'You have two choices,' he said silkily. 'One—you come back of your own volition. Two—I pick you up and carry you back.' He watched her with icy grey eyes. 'Take your pick.'

She looked up, her eyes flashing bright blue. 'You wouldn't . . .' she began.

'Yes?' he drawled, his fingers biting her skin. 'Do go on.' The dark brows rose. 'I'm fascinated.'

She bent her head, her mouth tight. 'They're not choices at all,' she muttered.

Nick shrugged lazily. 'They're all you're going to get from me. I shouldn't hesitate too long—I'm a very impatient man,' and he smiled, alarming her.

She felt her heart beat out a slow, desperate rhythm as she walked with him to the exit. As they walked out of the electric doors, her head swung, a frown marring her brow. 'My cases . . .' she began, looking towards the airways desk.

'I'll handle it.' His voice was brusque, his fingers punitive as he led her to where the long sinister limousine waited. He handed her into the front seat and slid in beside her. She had half expected him to have arrived with half a dozen strong-armed men, all standing menacingly around the car, but he was alone.

She watched him start the engine, his strong hand closing over the gear, his long legs pressing on the foot pedals. He looked incredible sexy driving the car, and she looked away, feeling her pulses leap with intense attraction towards him.

'Of course,' Nick drawled as they drove on to the freeway, 'with Tonino out like a light you'll have to put up with my driving.' He glanced at her, the overhead lights of the road flashing on to his face, gold running along his cheekbones, startling her with the sinister aspect of his features silhouetted against the bright lights.

They drove in tense silence. Olivia felt her nerves coil up like barbed wire as they sped back into the city, the tyres screeching at corners, the car swinging violently as they met with red lights. Nick was in a bad temper; she felt the tension increase.

'Get out of the car,' Nick told her as they screeched

to a halt outside his apartment.

She opened her door, standing on the sidewalk while he strode round to where she stood.

'Inside,' he ordered, taking her arm and hustling her into the foyer, straight to the lift. They got in and he pressed the button, turning to her with a cold expression, the lines of cheek and jaw aggressive, solid bone, making her swallow, her throat tightening.

'Is Tonino all right?' she asked, afraid to stand in silence any longer, needing to speak to clear the air.

Nick's mouth curled. 'Apart from the fact that he's dead to the world, yes, he's all right.' His hand bit into her arm as he pulled her out of the lift and into his apartment. 'But he's going to have a nasty headache in the morning.'

Olivia bit her lip, her hands clinging together. 'I didn't think,' she said anxiously. Poor Tonino, she thought, frowning.

'No?' he drawled tightly.

She looked up as he closed the door behind him. 'It was a split-second decision,' she pointed out irritably, 'I had to take the risk.'

He came towards her. 'Risk is right,' he said, his eyes burning on her, 'because let me tell you, lady, you've pushed me just a little bit too far this time!'

She swallowed, her throat tightening. 'You left me no choice,' she said, backing away a little until he was at a safe distance. 'There's no way I'm going to Sicily with you, and you'd better accept that now.'

'I accept nothing!' he ground between his teeth, and she fell silent for a moment at the violence in his tone.

'Be reasonable, for God's sake!' she said angrily, her hands clenching at her sides.

'I've been reasonable,' said Nick under his breath, and his voice hardened as he went on, 'I've been patient with you, I've kept my temper.' His jaw clamped together and he shook his head, 'Well, I'm not going to play the gentleman any more for you!'

Her temper flared, her eyes flashing, hating him bitterly. 'You're not a gentleman,' she said angrily. 'You've done nothing but push me around ever since I set eyes on you.'

His eyes leapt with temper. 'You paid your money and you took your choice,' he said bitingly. 'You knew what you were doing, and you knew how I'd react.'

Olivia backed away for a couple of steps, and her back came into contact with the open door of her bedroom. 'I don't care what you say,' she snapped, 'I am not going to Sicily!'

Nick's eyes flared, leaping with controlled anger. 'My brother . . .' he began, but she cut him off with a bitter laugh:

'Oh, don't start that again, please!' Her eyes hated him as she faced him across the room. 'You don't care a damn about your brother. You just want to punish me!'

His hands clenched and unclenched at his sides. 'Why the hell should I want to do that?'

'Because you want me, and you hate yourself for it!' she shouted, then caught her breath, her hands flying to her face as she stared at him in horror.

His eyes were black with rage. 'You bitch!' he bit out, and suddenly he was coming for her, pushing furniture out of the way violently, his face filled with manic rage.

Olivia tried to run into her bedroom and close the door behind her, but he crashed it back and she gasped, edging away from him. 'Please . . .' she begged in breathless panic, her hands up against his attack, 'I didn't mean . . .'

His hands clamped on her shoulders and he dragged her towards him, his eyes leaping with fury. His mouth clamped on hers in a biting ruthless kiss, forcing her lips back against her teeth until she felt she could no longer stand the assault. She tried to push him away, her hands beating on his chest, her breath coming in gasps. Nick pushed her back until her knees hit the edge of the bed.

'No!' she cried, her voice throbbing with panic. His hands gripped her wrists above her head as he pushed her down into the bed, bending over her with a furious expression.

'Shut up!' he bit out, and his head bent to kiss her brutally, hurting her as his fingers bit into her. She struggled, writhing beneath him, her body bucking and jerking while he deliberately tried to hurt her.

Then something strange happened. One minute they were fighting, the next they were clinging together in an urgent flare of passion. Nick's mouth clung to hers as he kissed her with an intensity that made her buckle in heat, her breasts heaving.

Her hands tangled in his hair, as she kissed him back with intensity, her body moulding its soft contours to his as they pressed tightly together, holding on to each other, as though they were drowning.

His hands gripped her head, his mouth burning on hers, their hearts racing together as the fire built inside them and they clung in frenzied, heated pleasure.

Nick raised his head, his breathing unsteady, his face flushed. They stared at each other, in confusion, their faces filled with heated colour, their hearts racing as they struggled to breathe.

'My God,' Nick muttered thickly, his eyes glittering black with desire, and he stared down at her.

Olivia stared wide-eyed, her pulses skidding and thudding crazily. His black head bent again and she gasped, her hands going to his shoulders to try to push him away.

'All right!' she said breathlessly, bewildered and shocked by the flame which had burnt between them. 'You win—I'll come to Sicily!' She was desperately trying to stop him kissing her again, but it didn't work.

'Too right I win,' he muttered thickly, 'and the winner takes it all.' His head swooped, taking her mouth, parting her lips beneath his while his hands slid sensually down her body, making her writhe against him, her heart racing out of control.

His hands closed over her breasts and she groaned feverishly, her mind totally wiped out by the powerful force of his kiss. He undid her blouse with strong hands which shook just a little, and slipped his hand inside, pulling her blouse apart.

He raised his head to look down at her white exposed breasts and a deep groan came from his throat, a growl that made her shiver as his head bent to her neck. His hot mouth burned a trail over her throat to the base of her neck where a pulse beat crazily, his tongue snaking out over her skin until she moaned, her head twisting from side to side.

Her fingers twisted in his hair as his mouth moved to her breasts, his strong white teeth biting her gently, making her catch her breath with dizzy confusion. His tongue snaked out across her burning nipple, and the throbbing heat shot up higher, her breath coming like a steam train. He came back to take her mouth again, his long fingers moving frenziedly over her breast while he kissed her.

Olivia felt his other hand move to the panel of her stomach and she stiffened, her mind coming back with a loud NO, and she tried to twist away, shaking, her whole body trembling.

She cried out, pushing away from him, meeting his black heated gaze with a shiver.

His hand fell to her breast. He groaned from deep in his throat. 'Yes,' he said thickly, and his long fingers made her buckle, shivering with deep arousal.

But her mind won out over the liquid heat that was flooding her body. With an almighty push of desperation, she shoved him away from her, leaping up off the bed, her breath coming in gasps as she sought to control herself and stand at ease.

Nick began to get up and follow her. 'Don't!' she said, her voice high with panic, holding her hands up against him. 'Please don't!' Her legs were shaking, her whole body trembling and she felt that her knees might give way at any moment.

Nick's eyes burned into her soul. 'We go well together,' he said thickly, and he reached for her. 'You're right—I do want you.' His hands closed over her shoulders and he pulled her to him, 'I want you very badly.'

Olivia swallowed, her cheeks hot and flushed. 'But I don't want you. I don't want anything to do with you.'

His eyes darkened. 'Don't lie,' he muttered, catching her chin and tilting her head back. 'You felt it too.'

She shook her head desperately. 'No,' she moaned, her voice low and throbbing, 'you forced me into it.'

His fingers tightened on her chin, eyes narrowing. 'There's something between us. You felt it when I kissed you—you can't deny it. I almost went up in flames and so did you.'

Tears stung her eyes and she shook her head again. 'It isn't right,' she said breathlessly, closing her eyes.

'Listen to me,' he said deeply, his voice hoarse, 'I'll give you anything you want. I'm a very generous man, I've told you before. Let me love you, Olivia, and I'll get you anything you ask for.'

Her eyes flew open, staring at him as the heat left her body, leaving her filled with incredulous rage as his words sunk home, spinning in her mind. He couldn't have chosen a better way to insult her, or to make her hate him.

'Get out of my room!' she ground between her teeth, and stared at him, hatred and dislike in her eyes.

Nick was silent for a moment, watching her with narrowed eyes. 'I don't get it,' he said harshly, his face tightening. 'You were with me all the way back there—I felt it. You practically melted, the same way I did!'

Her mouth hardened into an angry, bitter line, her cheeks flushing with hot colour. 'Listen to me, Mr Baretta,' she said in a cold icy voice, 'and listen to me good. If you ever lay a finger on me again, I'll kill you!'

He watched her in a bitter hostile silence for a moment. Then he pushed her away from him, his eyes furious, and stormed out of the room, slamming the door after him.

Olivia took several deep breaths, then felt the hot tears squeeze their way out of her lids, flowing down her cheeks while she cried in total silence, not making a sound, biting her lip, her eyes tightly closed while the tears burned on her cheeks.

Slowly she sat down on the bed, staring at nothing, her face blank, without thought. The tears subsided, but she didn't move. She just sat there for heaven knew how long, unable to think, unable to move, just sitting alone in silence, trying to control herself.

The kiss had devastated her. It had pushed back every barrier she had, made her realise just how much she was attracted to him. He was right, she had been with him all the way, she had felt it too. She had just been incredulous at the power.

Nick had crashed his way through her barriers with one fell swoop, and she didn't know how to handle it. The intensity had leapt between them like an electric shock, shattering her preconceptions about him and about herself, making her feel as though someone had lit a fuse attached to her.

She must never let him near her again. There was something very powerful between them. But she knew that as far as Nick was concerned it wasn't love, and that meant only one thing. He wanted her badly, yes— but he only wanted her to make love to him.

Hadn't he already told her? He wanted to fall into her bed, not her heart.

CHAPTER SIX

SHE avoided Nick's eyes the next morning. She felt his burning gaze beating into her, but whenever she looked round she couldn't hold his eyes, and she dropped her own away from him, flushing hotly as memories of the previous night came back to her. They had breakfast separately, their faces expressionless when they looked at each other, silence hanging between them like a black raincloud.

At midday, there was a sound from the hall. They both looked up at the same moment. Nick got out of his chair, walking across to the door which led to Tonino's room and disappearing inside it while Olivia stayed where she was.

She bit her lip, looking at her hands. Poor Tonino! She didn't know quite what she could say to him. She wondered whether he would be angry with her. She wouldn't blame the poor man. She wouldn't enjoy being slipped a couple of pills in her drink.

A few minutes later Tonino came out, walking with slow steps, his face creased, his hands up against his head.

Olivia watched him sit agonisingly down in a chair, groaning a little. 'Hello, Tonino,' she said quietly, her face anxious as she watched him, afraid that he wouldn't speak to her.

Tonino looked up. 'Oh no!' he groaned, pressing his fingers to his scalp. 'Is the Mafia lady with the thin Mickey!'

Olivia frowned, perplexed. 'Thin Mickey?'

'Sure,' he mumbled, 'when you slip a little something in some poor guy's drink.'

She felt a smile curve her lips and checked it, looking at him with affection. '—I think you mean a Mickey Finn,' she said, amused.

'My English!' he laughed, his eyes bright for a second. 'Is terrible!' Then he groaned, his hands going to his temples. 'No laughing, please. Is bad for my head.'

She bit her lip. 'I'm sorry, Tonino, really I am,' she said anxiously, and leaned forward to lay a gentle hand on his arm. 'I didn't realise it would knock you out like that.' She frowned, worried. 'How bad is it?'

'Pretty goddamned bad,' he mumbled, closing his eyes briefly and clutching his head with long fingers. 'But is all right, I forgive you. Now, can I have a coffee, please?'

She nodded, standing up. 'Wait there,' she said gently, going into the kitchen and reheating the coffee. She put it in a cup and brought it into the living room.

Tonino looked up as she handed it to him. 'Er,' he said, 'hold on. Let me see you taste it first—make me feel a whole lot safer.'

Olivia smiled, her cheeks dimpling, then raising the cup, she drank. 'See? Just coffee.' She handed it to him and said, 'It'll make you feel better.'

Tonino raised dark brows. 'Is pretty big miracle if it does,' he commented, sipping the coffee and leaning back in the chair with a groan, his eyes closing, his dark face smoothing out in relaxation.

Nick came into the room looking dangerously sexy in a casual outfit of tight black jeans and a well-fitting black sweater, his tanned throat and upper chest exposed by the V-neck. He thrust his hands into his pockets, eyeing her with a controlled face, the steel grey eyes burning through her.

'I have a lot to clear up before we leave tomorrow,' he said flatly. 'Unfinished business always makes me angry.'

Olivia flushed, getting the hidden implications at once. 'Okay,' she said huskily, 'I'll be here with Tonino. I don't think he should be left on his own anyway.'

'You'd better pack to leave tomorrow,' he told her, watching her from beneath hooded lids, his face unreadable. 'We're picking Greg up from the hospital at seven a.m., and flying straight on to Palermo.'

She nodded. 'I'll be ready.'

Nick hesitated, about to say something else, then he turned on his heel and walked to the door, turning his black head to look over his shoulder for a second.

'Be here when I get back,' he said tightly, and went out, closing the door with a sharp click behind him.

Olivia looked down, biting her lip. Then she put her face in her hands and sighed. What on earth was she going to do?

She had expected the sun to shine in welcome. But the skies were dark as they flew over Sicily. The gods were against her, darkening the heavens and clouding the sky.

The landscape seemed ever more dramatic, more forbidding. Harsh, jagged mountains clawed their way to the sky, their slopes decked in green bushes, the splashes of colourful red flowers dampened by rain. The wild, untameable scenery seemed threatening, defiant as the rough wind blew over the hills and mountains, making the dark bushes ruffle and dance against it.

It seemed an ominous day to arrive in Sicily, and Olivia's face was pale as her eyes scanned the landscape below.

Greg pressed his hand on hers. 'We're home,' he murmured beside her, and the warmth in his voice made her turn her head.

She smiled, her face tense. Guilt flowed through her and she found she couldn't meet his eyes. He still believed she had come to his home with him to marry him.

'Is this Palermo?' she asked, changing the subject deftly.

Greg glanced out of the window of the red and white private plane. 'Yes, it's the capital,' he told her.

The stark bare houses of the old quarter rose up, the patched and peeling stucco walls dampened to a dingy grey as the rain fell heavily on them. It looked as though it was caught in the grip of time. It could have been a medieval town, primeval, ruled by a feudal lord.

They landed at Punta Raisi Airport, a few kilometres outside Palermo, and once again a limousine awaited them. As they stepped into it, the wind whistled around their heads, the rain beat against their faces.

'We picked a bad day,' Nick said once the car door was shut firmly against the battery of elements.

Greg laughed. 'Typical!' he said, turning to look at Olivia. She noticed the hospital pallor on his face. 'Never mind—the sun will come out soon. It always does.'

Olivia smiled gently, listening to the beating on the roof of the car as the needles of rain hit it. 'Maybe Sicily doesn't like me,' she joked, looking at him sideways.

There was a little pause, then Nick drawled sardonically, 'There's an idea.' He flicked his dark gaze to her face without further comment.

She sat in between Greg and Nick in the back of the black limousine. Greg talked cheerfully as they drove across the rough, wild terrain towards Solunto.

He didn't notice the air of tension between Nick and Olivia. He didn't notice the dangerous silence between them. He didn't notice the way electricity crackled in the air whenever their eyes met. But Tonino noticed. He watched them with his dark, solemn eyes and said nothing.

'We're home,' said Greg after many miles of driving. The car crawled off the road up a long dusty track that led to two tall sunbleached stone gates. 'The Palazzo Baretta,' he added as the house came into view.

It rose before them—a massive stone edifice surrounded by wild bushes, trees and an air of dramatic nobility. Set on the upward slopes of Solunto, it towered imperiously over the village below. Carved figures peered down at them from the battlement rooftops. The family crest was placed above the great doors in the centre.

'What do you think?' Greg asked proudly as they stepped from the car.

Three men stood watching, silently, their silhouettes vague and sinister beside the house. Olivia looked back at Greg. 'It's remarkable,' she said, unable to sum up the beauty of it in any other way.

The storm had quietened, but the skies were still grey. As they approached the house they heard excited voices from within and the great doors were flung open.

'Gregorio!'

Greg's hand left Olivia's. 'Simonetta!' he exclaimed, his face breaking into a grin.

A young woman ran down the steps, a bright ribbon flowing from her lustrous brown hair. Her face was round, olive-skinned, her eyes a huge flashing black. She looked like a sensual self-indulgent Persian cat.

'*Ciao!*' she said, her full mouth pouting as she looked at him. '*Ciao*, Gregorio!' She flung herself on him, her arms around his neck.

Greg kissed her on both cheeks, and gently disentangled her. '*Inglese*, Simonetta,' he told her. 'We have an English guest.' He indicated Olivia a few steps behind him.

Simonetta's black eyes turned on her. Shock was reflected in her face, her eyes widening. Then they narrowed, and Olivia almost heard her purr with throaty dislike.

'Hello, Simonetta,' said Olivia, smiling.

Simonetta hesitated, then she nodded, the mane of silky brown hair rippling. '*Buon giorno,*' she said, showing even white teeth.

Olivia's eyes met Nick's. She frowned, looking away for a moment. Her eyes fell on the three men who stood watching and she half-turned to look back at Nick, a question on her lips.

'Shall we go in?' Nick suggested before she spoke, and Olivia was immediately distracted.

Simonetta wound her arm through Greg's. 'I be your nurse while you are here,' she said, and the flashing black eyes were shy, yet knowing. 'Is okay?'

Greg's smile was gentle. 'Olivia's my nurse,' he told her softly.

Simonetta stiffened, then she flicked her gaze to Olivia and held it for a long moment. Slowly she disengaged her arm from Greg's and began to walk into the house alone. Her voluptuous body, encased in a tightly-fitting purple dress, swayed with feline sensuousness.

'What's the matter with her?' asked Greg, watching her leave with dignity. 'Oh, I suppose I'd better go after her,' and he followed her quickly into the house.

'Welcome to my castle,' drawled a voice in Olivia's ear, and she turned as Nick's hand curled on her arm. They walked up the stone steps and crossed the threshold of the Palazzo Baretta together.

The stone baronial hall echoed with the understated power which hung around Nick himself. The walls were rough stone, covered with tapestries, patched with age, threads creeping from the edges, and richly coloured carpets covered the floor.

Olivia had never seen either of the Baretta brothers in their native surroundings. She had never imagined them to be so feudal, so awe-inspiring. The image of their family home had been of a Mediterranean villa, not an ancestral *palazzo*.

She took a step towards the great staircase. 'Are these your ancestors?' she asked, her voice echoing in the cool hall.

Nick came to stand beside her. 'Motley crew, aren't they?' he drawled, and ran one long finger over the surface of the richly painted oil canvas of the portrait.

She shivered as she stepped on to the next portrait. 'He looks like you,' she said quietly, staring at the same sinister grey eyes, the same uncompromising features.

Nick's smile turned her blood to ice. 'He was a murderer,' he murmured in her ear.

She eyed him coolly. 'Runs in the family, does it?'

He raised dark brows with offence, and there was a long silence. Then he gave her a slow, icy smile. 'Any man is capable of murder,' he told her, 'with the right provocation.'

Her eyes were riveted on him. 'Which is?'

Nick shrugged lazily, the broad shoulders fitting perfectly beneath his dark jacket. 'Women tend to be the greatest motive.'

Olivia held his gaze for a long moment, then she looked away, running her hands softly over the gilt frame of the portrait. She noticed the seventeenth-century clothes the man in the portrait wore, and frowned.

'How long has this place been in your family?'

His face darkened, becoming brooding. 'That's a long story,' he said, and the long fingers closed over her chin, while he regarded her with narrowed eyes. 'I'll tell you about it one day. But not yet.'

She raised her brows. 'A rich past?' she asked huskily.

'Very,' he agreed, and a cool smile touched his hard mouth. 'You could almost say—a legacy of violence.'

She shivered, the tremendous impact of sinister danger making a sharp frisson of alarm run down her spine. She stared at him in silence, incapable of answering.

'Careful, Nick!' A calm, female Italian voice brought her out of her thoughts. She turned. 'You'll give her nightmares!'

The woman was about fifty, her hair a mass of black

and silver, her olive skin criss-crossed with lines. The round dark eyes that studied Olivia were knowing, wise. The woman was slender, her tall body encased in the best Italian silk.

Nick walked over to her with a brief smile. 'I think she'll survive, Mamma,' he said lazily, and pressed his firm mouth to her cheeks three times. 'You used to tell me terrible tales of Sicily when I was a boy.'

His mother laughed, clasping tanned hands together, rings flashing from every finger. 'Ah, but you had terrible nightmares to match. And I used to rock you to sleep afterwards.'

Nick's mouth curved in a slow, lazy smile. 'How do you know I don't rock Miss Courtney to sleep?'

Signora Baretta raised her brows. 'Because if you did, you certainly wouldn't call her Miss Courtney,' she pointed out in a throaty voice. She turned to look at Olivia, her face thoughtful, considering. Olivia felt she could lose herself in those silent, black eyes. They were filled with deep wisdom and strength.

'You must be Olivia,' said Signora Baretta, her silk skirt rustling at her legs as she came towards her. 'Let me look at you.' She took her hands and held her at arm's length, studying her thoughtfully. A fragrance as warm as summer surrounded her. 'Why, you could almost be Sicilian with all that dark hair. Your eyes are a little too blue, your skin too pale, but . . .' she gave an elegant shrug, smiling. 'It is there. Welcome to my home.'

'I'm glad to meet you at last, Signora Baretta,' Olivia said, smiling, 'I've heard a lot about you.'

'Oh?' The shrewd dark eyes lifted to Nick's face for a second. Then she smiled again. 'You must call me

Maria. I too have heard a great deal about you. From
. . .' she eyed Nick, 'both my sons.'

'Really?' Olivia looked at Nick too. He stared back at
her with narrowed grey eyes, his expression unreadable.

Maria Baretta noted this with a shrewd expression.
'There is nothing of the Mediterranean about you,
Nick,' she commented, half-smiling at the cool look on
his face. She turned back to Olivia. 'Sometimes I think I
let my boys become too American.'

She had a sudden image of Nick in a violent temper
and couldn't agree. 'Oh,' she replied, raising her brows
wryly, 'I think he has more than his fair share of Latin
characteristics!' Nick was hardly what she would call
cold-blooded.

Signora Baretta laughed with wicked delight. 'So!' she
said, her dark eyes glinting, 'you've come up against his
famous temper, have you? My dear, we have so much in
common!'

Nick's mouth indented. 'No plots, please, Mama,' he
drawled, his hands sliding into his pockets.

'My son believes me to be a devious woman,' Maria
Baretta told Olivia with slightly narrowed eyes. She
wound her arm through hers and began to lead her into
the main room of the house. 'Quite ridiculous! Would
you like some cake? A glass of Marsala, perhaps?'

Olivia gave Nick a sideways glance beneath her lashes
as she passed him. The main room was bigger than the
hall, with the same rough-hewn stone walls, pictures
hanging, the rich carpet on the floor a deep blood red,
polished wood furniture gleaming.

'It is sweet but refreshing,' Signora Baretta told her,
handing her a glass of the rich dessert wine, the crystal
glass clinking as it touched her fingernails. 'We have

given up our *siesta* for you!' she smiled, raising her brows, 'so the least you can do is drink with us.'

Olivia took the glass, and chinked it against Signora Baretta's in a silent toast. She was grateful for the warm hospitality. Sicilians were famed for their extensive hospitality—when a guest was welcome. If he or she wasn't welcome, they were in for cold, abrupt silence. But Olivia felt at ease with this woman with the dark eyes. She felt she could trust her.

Simonetta had wound herself insiduously around Greg like a sleek serpent, her gaze intense as she looked at him. Greg patted her head absently, and Olivia watched the girl's face darken.

'Like it?' Greg asked her, and Olivia looked up with a smile.

'It's delicious,' she said, nodding. Nick was watching them with a cold expression, his eyes narrowing as he watched the close, easy friendship between them.

Greg put his own glass down and came over to her. 'You like my girl, Mamma?' he asked Signora Baretta as he took Olivia's hands in his and kissed the top of them tenderly.

Signora Baretta shot a quick glance at Nick, and an amused smile played on her lips. 'She is beautiful, Gregorio,' she agreed, and looked sideways at her eldest son. 'Don't you agree, Nick?' she said softly.

There was a little silence in the room. Olivia straightened, her eyes darting to Nick. His face was cold, hostile as he watched her and she felt her throat tighten.

'Beautiful,' Nick drawled, and she heard the icy note in his tone.

Olivia flushed, stiffening. She looked across the room towards the large wooden shutters that were flung open and saw the sun come filtering through the clouds outside.

'The storm's over,' she said shakily, detracting attention from herself and Nick. The garden had lit up in a dizzying array of colour. The grass was a dazzling green bleached yellow in parts, the bright pink bougainvillaea a splash of colour against the olive-green shrubs and trees.

'That is good!' Signora Baretta sipped a little wine and sighed. 'The men in the village will be safe now. They didn't go out this morning,' she addressed this to Nick, 'since eight o'clock.' She nodded and repeated, 'Eight o'clock! The storm started early enough to warn them, thank God.'

Olivia shifted while Greg sat down beside her, still holding her hand. 'Are they all fishermen in the village?' she asked, knowing the extent of the Sicilian fishing industry. As it was an island, Sicily was renowned for its vast selection of fresh fish.

Signora Baretta nodded with a wry smile. 'What else is there for them to do? Living so close to the sea, it is easier for them.' She shrugged. 'They would feel trapped in city life. They are free men here—but how their women suffer when the sea turns against them!'

Greg was stroking Olivia's hand absently, and she frowned as she saw Simonetta's eyes flash a malevolent black. She tilted her head to one side, watching the girl thoughtfully.

Nick pushed away from the wall abruptly. 'I'll show Olivia her room,' he said, coming towards her at a slow, laconic pace. She looked away as her gaze strayed to his long, powerful legs.

Greg gave a weak laugh. 'I should do that!' he complained.

Nick flicked his glance to him briefly. 'You should be in bed,' he said flatly. He took Olivia's wrist, and she stood up silently, following him to the oak door. His tanned hand closed round the brass handle, the black hairs weaving a little network on his wrist.

They climbed the stairs, past the menacing array of hot-blooded Sicilian ancestors, and Olivia looked away from those piercing eyes as they passed the portraits. They give me the shivers, she thought with a frown.

Down a narrow corridor they walked, side by side, their heels clicking discreetly on the stone floor until Nick stopped at a door, opened it and led her in. The room was bright and airy, the bed dominating it with a pretty blue and white flowered bedspread. The shutters were closed at the large window.

'My lady's chamber,' Nick drawled, going over to the shutters and flinging them wide open. The bright golden sun framed him in the window, his black hair shining, his eyes almost silver, making him seem like a deadly angel—haloed by gold but lethal.

'It's lovely!' Olivia's hands clasped together, suddenly nervous in his presence, feeling the undercurrent of controlled sexual violence which was so strong a part of his attraction. 'Thank you.' She looked at him with a straight face.

Nick leaned on the windowsill, his arms folded, his body lazy. 'What do you think of Simonetta?' he asked.

She frowned, puzzled. 'She seems very nice,' she said, thinking again how much Simonetta reminded her of a silent Persian cat. Her eyes were the most powerful thing, she decided thoughtfully; they were magnetic.

One dark brow rose sardonically. 'Don't tell me you

haven't noticed?' he asked.

'Noticed what?' She tilted her head to one side, uneasy under that piercing stare. 'That's she's extremely beautiful? Yes, I noticed that.'

Nick watched her for a moment, then said, 'Not very perceptive, are you?' He rested one hand on the ledge of the window, his fingers strongly defined against the white-painted wood. 'Simonetta has known Greg for a long time.'

'I can see that,' she said, feeling the nervous tension increase at the look in his eyes, 'I don't need to be perceptive to see that they're good friends.' She raised her brows, watching him.

Nick's mouth indented. 'More than good friends, I think,' he said, sliding one hand in his pocket.

Nerves made her laugh. 'Very good friends?' she asked, laughing, and instantly regretted it.

There was a little silence, then his grey eyes narrowed on her. 'Do you find me amusing, Miss Courtney?' he asked in a tight, menacing voice.

She shivered, coming back down to earth from her nervous humour. 'I'm just a little tense,' she told him quietly, and shrugged. 'I was making a joke.'

'At my expense?' he asked dangerously.

She felt her throat tighten. 'I thought we were talking about Simonetta.'

He watched her for a brief moment, then he relaxed, inclining his black head and taking a cigar from his inside jacket pocket. She breathed a sigh of silent relief. The gold lighter flared and tendrils of smoke wound from the glowing tip of the cigar around Nick's dark face.

'Simonetta's parents died when she was twelve,' he

continued. 'My mother took her in, and for the last eight years she's lived here.' He paused and a wry smile touched his mouth. 'I think she sees me as a father figure,' he said, shrugging. 'Not very flattering, but there you have it.'

Olivia watched him. 'And how does she see Greg?' she asked slowly.

The grey eyes flicked to hers. 'She's in love with him.'

'Oh . . .' She couldn't think of anything to say. She remembered the shock on Simonetta's face when she first arrived. I should have realised then, she thought with a heavy sigh, I should have understood. Simonetta had almost gone back on all fours in an arch and hissed at her from the moment she had arrived at the house.

She looked up at Nick, suddenly very angry. 'Why didn't you tell me before?' she asked, her mouth tightening. He had put her in a difficult situation. Simonetta might get hurt because of her.

'Would it have made any difference?' he asked coolly, raising one brow. 'You would still have been here, and she would still have loved him.'

Olivia looked away, biting her lip. 'It's going to make things very difficult for both of us,' she said. Her eyes focussed on the gleaming polished wood floor.

'How sad,' Nick said tightly,' 'that's really tragic. It must be heartbreaking to realise you have competition.'

Her head came back at that, her eyes fixing on him with bitter anger. 'What do you mean, competition?' she asked through tight, pale lips. 'I've told you, I'm not marrying your brother.'

He laughed under his breath, and her blood turned to ice. 'So you have,' he said through his teeth, and his eyes narrowed. 'Maybe you're not convincing enough. Try harder.'

Her mouth tightened in a firm angry line as she stared bitterly at him. 'What do I have to do—write it down for you in blood?'

He was silent for a moment. Then he said very softly, 'Don't challenge me, Olivia. You'll regret it.'

He pushed away from the window. The sun flashed in her eyes, blinding her for a moment as his shadow moved towards her. Then he moved back, blocking out the sun, and she saw how close he was to her, felt her pulses leap at his nearness.

Nick ran a comprehensive eye over her. 'You think she'll let you get away with it?' he asked, raising one brow, 'let you steal him from under her nose?' He smiled, showing sharp white teeth, and shook his head. 'No way. She'll put up one hell of a fight.'

'She doesn't need to,' she told him, ignoring the way her heart thudded too fast as she stood so close to him. 'I have no intention of stealing him—you know that as well as I do.'

'I know this,' said Nick in a menacing voice, his hand reaching out to grasp a handful of her hair, his long fingers tangling in the glossy black locks, 'you're a very clever woman. But not clever enough. I won't let my brother make a fool of himself over you.'

'Won't you?' she gritted between her teeth. Her neck was hurting as he jerked it back farther.

His smile was chilling. 'You've met your match with me,' he said, and she heard the silky menace in his tone, making her shiver with alarm. 'I'm nobody's fool.'

She tried to jerk away from him, suddenly frightened of the way her body was reacting to him. Her knees felt weak, her pulses skidding crazily inside her, her heart thudding.

'I don't want your brother!' she said in a low voice, gasping as he pulled her back to him until she landed against his chest.

His eyes darkened as he looked down at her. 'No,' he said under his breath, and she felt herself sway against him, 'because you want me.'

She stared at him. Their eyes met and fused, and her knees almost buckled at the animal predatory look she saw in his eyes. 'I don't want anything to do with you,' she said, lying shakily.

'No?' he said thickly, and one hand slid to her throat as he stepped closer. 'Convince me.'

His black head descended slowly, and she watched, her heart hammering faster until it shot out of control as his mouth took hers in a warm, coaxing kiss until her eyes closed helplessly.

The control was breathtaking. He kissed her slowly, drawing away languorously, then coming back to kiss her again, his lips warm, teasing, filling her with a burning sensuality that made her mind spin, until she kissed him back, then he drew away again, leaving her swaying against him, needing to feel the full impact of that hard mouth.

Then his arms slid round her tightly, pressing her against his hard body, while his hot mouth moved urgently on hers, his fingers biting into her waist while she arched against him, her hands twining around his neck, tangling in his thick black hair.

He raised his head, his eyes glittering down at her, his face flushed. 'You see?' he murmured thickly. 'You want me as much as I want you—admit it.'

Olivia swayed unsteadily, and his hands slid to hold her upright. She was confused and upset, her face flushed, her breathing disturbed. How did he manage to affect her like this? His touch hit her like a thunderbolt every time he came near her.

'Don't Nick,' she said with difficulty, her voice husky as she avoided his eyes.

'It works both ways, Olivia,' he muttered, lifting her hand to his mouth, his lips tracing each finger, each mound of her palm with breathtakingly sensual control. 'You knock me off balance too. Don't you know what you do to me? It's something pretty drastic. I'd give you anything you asked for if you let me make love to you.' His eyes darkened on her mouth. 'Anything!'

She stiffened, feeling the ice spread slowly over her body, staring at him with intense dislike. 'You couldn't give me anything I'd want,' she said through her teeth, her back rigid.

He frowned, his eyes narrowing. He was about to speak, his lips parting, but there was a sharp rap at the door.

'I got the lady's case, boss,' Tonino's voice came from outside.

Nick leant over irritably and opened the door. 'Put it over there,' he told Tonino, who came in and looked at Olivia's confused face silently, before he turned back to Nick.

'Signora Baretta wants you downstairs,' he told Nick.

Nick muttered something under his breath, then he raked a hand through his hair. 'Hell!' he muttered, throwing Olivia a brief glance before striding out of the room.

Tonino watched her with dark, silent eyes and she felt herself flush slowly. Bending her head, she walked quietly out of the room, her heels clicking on the stone corridor outside. Tonino followed her as she walked down the great oak stairs, lost in her thoughts.

She was suddenly glad she had telephoned her sister to let her know where she was staying. Tonino had refused to give her the address, but had given her the telephone number of the Palazzo Baretta instead.

Nick's attitude bewildered her. His feelings towards her seemed to be a terrible contradiction of love and rage. At one and the same time he wanted to both hurt her and make love to her—a dangerous combination, she thought grimly.

Her sister had been very worried when she told her she was going to Sicily. 'Sicily?' she had shrieked. 'They might cut off your left ear and post it through my letter box! I don't want to pay hundreds of pounds to get the rest of you back!' Olivia had laughed at the time. That hadn't worried her.

What did worry her was that Nick was taking an even closer interest in her now. It should have put her mind at rest, but strangely enough, it only worried her further.

Simonetta and Greg were nowhere to be seen when she walked into the room they had been in before. Nick stood by the wall, leaning lazily against it, his jacket slung over a chair, his white shirt open at the neck, exposing the tanned column of his throat, the beginning of his chest.

Tonino followed Olivia into the room, closing the door quietly behind him. 'Anyone seen Lala?' he asked in a casual voice.

Signora Baretta raised her head. 'She went shopping in the village,' she told him and Olivia could have sworn she detected an impish smile hovering around her mouth.

'Oh.' Tonino nodded, disappointed.

'Who's Lala?' Olivia leaned forward before Signora Baretta could speak.

Tonino watched her for a moment, then made a face. 'She's my girl,' he said, and sniffed, his face taking on an offended look, 'and she goes shopping when I come home!'

Signora Baretta laughed, clasping her hands in delight. 'She wanted to wait and see you, Nino,' she told him gently, her eyes dancing, 'but I sent her for fresh food for dinner tonight. She'll be back soon.'

Tonino watched her for a second, then his face broke into a monkeyish grin, his eyes lighting up with rueful humour. 'Is still not nice!' he complained, laughing. 'She is no good—I tell her so when she comes back.' He looked at them all, grinning away like mad, and said, 'No really, is true! I tell her . . .'

The doorknocker crashed into the silence as it hit the door outside, and Tonino broke off, looking at Nick, who pushed away from the wall, frowning, looking towards the hall.

'Who the hell is that?' Nick muttered under his breath.

The knocking grew louder, more urgent. Nick moved towards the door with the swift tread of a wolf. Tonino followed him as he wrenched open the door and they both went into the hall.

Rapid Italian voices spoke urgently in the hall, Olivia stood up slowly, trying to understand the words, but it was impossible—they were too fast, too staccato.

Olivia frowned, looking at Signora Baretta, studying

the deep brown eyes that watched her. 'What is it?' she asked. 'What's happening?'

Signora Baretta said simply, 'It is better to wait. They will tell us in their own time.'

Olivia didn't like the sound of that. Going across the room, she pulled the door quietly back and stepped into the hall, trying to read the men's frantic gestures as they spoke.

Nick turned, sensing her presence. 'What the hell are you doing?' he asked tensely, and Olivia swallowed at the look on his harsh face.

Tonino laid a calm hand on Nick's arm. 'She doesn't speak Italian,' he reminded him quietly, glancing at Olivia as he spoke.

Nick nodded, and turned back to Tonino. 'Look after her till I get back,' he told him, and to the men who stood in the doorway, 'Let's go!' They followed him as he walked swiftly into the bright sunlit garden, the crisp white of his shirt dazzling in the heat.

Olivia stared at Tonino in silence for a moment. Another burglary? No, Nick didn't have an offices in Sicily. Or did he? Perhaps he had some in Palermo—it was the capital, after all.

Tonino walked past her without a word, and Olivia frowned, watching him uneasily. She followed him into the other room, closing the door behind them quietly.

'What has happened?' Signora Baretta was waiting calmly for an explanation from him.

Tonino watched her in silence, then slid his hands in his pockets. 'Is Gina Rocco, in the village,' he told her, then paused, adding, 'Vincente Rocco's wife.'

Signora Baretta nodded slowly, her brow creasing with a frown. 'Vincente's wife?' she said slowly. 'But I know her—I know her well. What has happened to her?'

Tonino said very quietly, 'Vincente caught her in bed with another man. He's after them both.'

A gasp escaped Signora Baretta's lips, and she paled, staring at Tonino in horror.

CHAPTER SEVEN

OLIVIA couldn't bear the tension as they waited for Nick to return. Simonetta had come downstairs an hour after Nick had left, and had taken the news about Gina Rocco very badly. Gina was a good friend of hers, she said, she had known her for years. Olivia watched her worried face and felt her own tension increase.

In the end she couldn't bear it any longer. She went upstairs to see if Greg was all right. Simonetta had stayed with him until he was asleep, but Olivia thought he might wake up as it was daylight still, and might want someone to talk to.

He was still asleep when she arrived at his room. The windows were open, the white lace curtain rippling gently in the slight breeze from the sea over the hill. The sound of crickets buzzing and chirping outside broke the silence in the small oak room.

She tiptoed to his bed, looking down at his face, untroubled in sleep. The journey had obviously tired him out. She smoothed back a strand of light brown hair from his forehead affectionately, listening to the regular, steady sound of his breathing.

His lids fluttered open and he frowned. 'Olivia?' he said quietly. 'I thought Simonetta was with me. Where did she go?'

She smiled, stroking his forehead again gently. 'Don't worry,' she told him softly, 'she'll come back later. You go to sleep now, and rest.'

121

A tired sigh escaped his parted lips and he hesitated, then closed his eyes. The breeze stirred the curtains gently. Olivia watched him and smiled. Poor Greg! He was worn out. She tiptoed from the room, leaving him to sleep it off.

When she was half-way down the stairs she heard a footstep in the hall, and looking down she saw Nick. He was watching her with narrowed grey eyes, his expression controlled.

'Where have you been?' he asked slowly, then his glance followed the rest of the steps up. 'Upstairs? In your room?'

Olivia shook her head. 'I thought Greg might wake up. I thought he might want someone to talk to.'

His eyes narrowed further. 'Did you?' he said flatly, his body still. 'If I went up to bed now, would you come up to see if I wanted someone to talk to?' He thrust his hands in his pockets, his face hard. 'Or is that a different matter?'

She flushed, looking away. 'Greg's ill—you're not.' She walked the rest of the way down the stairs until she came to the foot of them, standing waiting for him to move out of her way.

'What you mean is . . .' Nick began, but broke off as the door to the main room opened. His head swung to look towards it irritably.

Signora Baretta came out, her face anxious. She looked at Nick, her round dark eyes enquiring. 'You came in the back way,' she stated, her body held still in apprehension. 'We were looking for you from the front.' Her eyes slowly moved to Olivia's face, then back to Nick's in silence. Then she asked, 'What happened? Is Gina all right?'

Nick nodded brusquely, his mouth compressed. 'I

found Vincente before he found her.'

Olivia tilted her head to one side, frowning. She heard Signora Baretta breathe a sigh of relief, her eyes closing as the lines of anxiety were smoothed from her olive-skinned face.

'What would he have done,' she asked them curiously, 'if he'd found her?'

Nick raised his brows slowly but did not reply.

Olivia looked away, unwilling to ask any more questions. Her hands nervously smoothed the folds of her white summer dress, and she bent her head, moving past Nick and his mother without another word. She walked into the main room, going past Tonino and Simonetta as they too appeared in the doorway, listening to Nick as he told them where he had found Vincente Rocco and sorted out the anger he felt towards his errant wife.

She didn't understand this country; she would be better off not thinking too hard about their customs. She sighed, looking out of the doors into the garden. The sun was setting into a warm, soothing afternoon lull. It had gradually lost its intense heat. The crickets were noisier now, buzzing and chirping merrily, invisible among the shrubs and bushes.

Olivia looked up as there was a knock on the door.

'That must be Giulia,' she heard Signora Baretta say with amusement, and then Tonino's footsteps went to the front door, opening it and chattering away in rapid cheerful Italian.

A few minutes later a girl appeared in the doorway, looking at Olivia.

'Hallo,' said the girl, coming into the room and offering Olivia a slim, elegant hand, 'you must be Olivia. I'm Giulia, Tonino's girl.'

'Hallo,' Olivia replied, puzzled.

She was a female replica of Tonino. Her face was bony, carved on a Roman structure, her nose hooked—seeming to lead the rest of her body as she moved. The great dark eyes were deep set, but instead of being solemn, like Tonino's, they were filled with laughter and light. Her hair was a pale brown, cut in flicks and layers around her face.

Olivia looked round as Tonino came into the room. 'I thought your name was Lala,' she said, hoping she wasn't being indiscreet.

The girl made a mock-offended face, her thin lips pulling in a smile. 'That Tonino!' she said, grinning, 'I think he is a no-good boy-friend. I'll get rid of him one day!'

Tonino laughed, his face lighting up in a monkeyish grin. 'Is because she sings,' he explained, 'all of the time, like this—La la la la la!'

Lala held a wicker basket under her arm, her slim body clothed in a pale blue dress which fitted her loosely. 'Dinner time soon,' she told Olivia, 'I must go and cook. I'll see you later.' She took Tonino's arm and began to lead him out to the kitchen. 'You can help me,' she told him firmly. Tonino nodded with a solemn expression and grinned at Olivia on his way out.

They disappeared out of the room and Olivia watched them with amusement. The perfect couple, she thought, smiling. They even looked like each other.

Dinner was served at eight. Olivia had changed into a cool white and green patterned dress which clung discreetly to her slender curves. As she walked into the long dining room she noticed Nick leaning casually against the long mantelpiece. He looked up as she walked in, and ran a comprehensive eye over her, noting the way her damp hair rested loosely around her shoulders, the metallic gleam of a gold necklace around her throat.

'Exquisite,' he murmured, and his gaze slid over her body. She felt as though he was stripping her indolently, removing her clothes with a flick of those grey eyes.

She gave him a polite smile, refusing to be ruffled. 'Thank you.' She walked calmly across the room to where he stood. 'Where are the others?'

Nick shrugged lazily, his black jacket fitting superbly over his shoulders. 'They'll be down.' He put his crystal glass down on the mantelpiece. 'Drink?'

She nodded. 'Something cool.'

Nick handed her a Martini a moment later. His long fingers brushed hers and she looked up, meeting his eyes with a jolt.

He raised one dark brow. 'You're jumpy tonight,' he drawled, and his eyes narrowed speculatively. 'What have you been up to?'

She shrugged. 'Nothing,' she told him, sipping her drink with a calm air.

He was watching her closely. 'Been to see Greg?' he asked in a lazy drawl.

Olivia looked at him slowly through her lashes and did not reply.

The other members of the family came down a moment later and filtered into the dining room. They took their places around the long polished wood table.

Nick sat at the head of the table. He was the head of the Baretta family. Olivia was to his right, and she felt distinctly uncomfortable as his steely gaze rested on her from time to time during the course of the meal.

Lala served the first course, *caponata,* a cold dish made from aubergines, capers, olives, tomatoes and celery. It looked peculiar at first, but Olivia found she liked it once she had got used to it.

'Poor Gina,' Signora Baretta was saying as they discussed at great length the misfortune of Gina Rocco and her lover in the village, 'it is very sad.'

'Poor Gina!' snorted Lala, wagging a bony finger. 'She likes the men too much, that is her big problem!'

Nick laughed under his breath. 'What you mean is,' he drawled lazily, flicking his glance towards her, 'the men like her too much. She's a very sexy lady.' He looked at Tonino. 'Don't you agree, Tonino?'

Tonino bit his lip, peeping at Lala. 'Well,' he said, spreading his hands expressively, his dark eyes filled with amusement, 'I don't like to say, boss.'

Olivia watched this with amusement, but felt a strange pang of irritation at Nick's remark. She allowed the conversation to float over her head, not wanting to get involved.

'Olivia,' Signora Baretta addressed her a moment later, 'I'm thinking of having a party soon for Greg. What do you think? Would you like that?'

There was a brief silence. Olivia could feel Nick's eyes burning into her, and frowned, putting her fork down slowly.

'It sounds lovely,' she said carefully, and looked at Nick for a second. His eyes were intent on her face, his body still as he watched her. She looked back at Signora Baretta worriedly. 'But shouldn't you ask Greg?'

She looked surprised. 'My dear,' she said, 'it will be your engagement party too.'

Olivia froze, and her eyes met Nick's in despair.

After dinner she escaped into the garden. The moon was glowing white against the dark blue night, silhouetting the branches of the trees, shining over the great stone gates of the house. The air was warm, the crickets chirping merrily, the occasional whine of a mosquito as it divebombed overhead.

She sighed, walking slowly until she reached a tree, then leaned against its trunk with a frown. Greg was planning to hold an engagement party for her, and Nick didn't seem about to step in on her behalf. Why should he? she thought irritably. He didn't seem to care one way or the other.

Her throat tightened. She could see the trap closing with every day she spent at this house. She felt angry towards Nick. She couldn't work him out. One moment he was against her marrying his brother, the next he was standing by and allowing her to get deeper and deeper into this whole mess.

She sensed him behind her at the same moment she smelt the cigar smoke. 'What do you want?' she asked, without turning round.

There was a silence. Then she heard Nick move closer to her, standing next to her. She watched silver-blue smoke drift past her as he drew on his cigar.

'What are you thinking about?' he asked suddenly.

She turned, throwing him an angry glance. 'What do you think?' Her eyes held his for a moment, then she looked away.

'Greg?' His voice was harsh, his eyes narrowed.

She nodded, her lashes sweeping her moonlit cheeks. 'Did you expect me to take it with a smile?'

Nick was watching her fixedly. 'I thought it was what you wanted,' he said, his voice strangely tense, 'to marry him. You should be pleased. It's being made easy for you.'

Her mouth compressed into a firm line. 'I won't argue with you,' she said under her breath, and turned, her eyes angry as she looked at him. 'There's no point, is there?'

He shook his black head and smiled slowly, making her blood boil. 'Very little,' he agreed in a maddening drawl. 'At least you're beginning to see that I'm not easily fooled.'

She was suddenly fed up with the whole thing. Pushing away from the tree, she said angrily, 'Forget it!' She began to walk away from him. 'I'm sick of going over the same pointless track with you!'

His hand snaked out, catching her wrist in an iron grip, and he whipped her back towards him, looking down into her angry, upturned face. They watched each other in a tense silence.

'All right,' Nick muttered, his eyes glittering beneath hooded lids, 'let's say I believe you. Then why did you push me away? If you don't want my brother, why wouldn't you let me make love to you?'

For a moment, Olivia was too angry with him for his conceit to reply. Then she controlled herself and said in a tight voice.

'Figure it out.' Her eyes ran over him with contempt and she raised her brows. 'It shouldn't be too difficult— unless of course your ego is bigger than your brain.'

His mouth tightened into an angry line, a red stain spreading over his angular cheekbones. His fingers bit into her wrist.

'That wasn't a very smart move, Miss Courtney,' he

said in a sinister threatening voice, and she saw the menace in his grey eyes. 'You would do well not to insult me. It'll only hurt you in the long run.'

'Why?' she asked, refusing to back down in the face of his threats. 'Don't you like hearing the truth?'

Nick's hand came up to her neck, the long fingers sliding over her throat, 'I'm a very dangerous enemy,' he said in an icy voice, and his fingers tightened around her throat. 'Be careful you don't provoke me.'

A frisson of alarm ran down her spine, making her shiver. 'You're hurting me,' she said in a low, frightened voice.

His smile was chilling. He thrust her head backwards, his teeth clamped tightly together as he watched her through narrowed, intent eyes. 'I could get to like hurting you,' he said tightly. 'There's something about you that brings out the animal in me.'

Her eyes met his. 'I've noticed,' she said without thinking.

'I'm glad to hear it,' he muttered between his teeth. 'I was beginning to think I wasn't getting through to you.'

Olivia stared at him in silence, and felt the rapid beat of her heart quicken, her pulses thudding in a captivating rhythm. Nick slid his hand over her wrist, and his eyes raised to hers as he felt the telltale beat of her pulse.

'I am getting through to you, aren't I?' he said thickly.

Olivia's heart skipped a beat at the look in his eyes. 'Yes,' she whispered, mesmerised.

He watched her intensely, then his hands drew her slowly towards him, his fingers sliding around her waist as he bent his black head, his mouth descending to hers. His lips brushed hers and her lids slowly closed as he teased her with his mouth for a few burning, agonising moments. Then they were clinging to each other, their mouths draining each other, while Nick's arms crushed her against him, moulding her body to his.

Her head spun and she reached out, her hands sliding on his hard chest, feeling the rapid thud of his heart, the heat of his flesh. His mouth burnt hers, his hands pressing into the small of her back as the kiss grew deeper, more urgent, the liquid pleasure overtaking them both with a rapidity and urgency that was frightening.

A halting footfall from the terrace made them draw apart, their faces flushed as they looked across the garden to the lighted house.

Simonetta stood watching them, her face incredulous, shocked. Olivia looked at Nick with a bitterness and longing that tore her apart, then turned and went back to the house, unable to look at Simonetta, aware that the other girl's eyes followed her with shocked amazement.

She went straight to her room and flung herself on the bed, breathing hard. Now Simonetta knew, and she would no doubt tell the rest of the family, unless Nick could dissuade her. Olivia gritted her teeth against the rise of humiliation inside her. Nick was thirty-seven and unmarried, and the obvious conclusions to be drawn were that he had never felt the need to marry. No doubt he always had too many women only too eager to go to bed with him until he tired of them.

She felt herself stiffen. That was what his family would think of her when they realised they were attracted to each other. Another of Nick's whims. She'll be gone soon, like all the rest.

Well, not me, Olivia thought angrily. I'll be damned if I'll give in to the swine! The sooner I get out of this mess the better.

And with that comforting thought, she locked her door, undressed, and went to sleep.

Nick was nowhere to be seen when she came down the following morning for breakfast. Simonetta passed her in the hall as she walked across it, and she found herself unable to look at the other girl. Simonetta said nothing, merely gave her an all-encompassing glance with those black eyes of hers and carried on walking.

Olivia's mouth tightened. Nick had really put her in a difficult situation. She went into the kitchen to see if anyone else was around.

'Morning!' Lala was hovering over the stove like a graceful sparrow when Olivia got into the kitchen. 'You sleep well?'

She nodded with a smile and moved to the table, sitting on one of the wooden chairs. 'Is this still fresh?' she asked, pointing to the coffee, and Lala nodded with a bright smile. Olivia poured herself a cup, then asked, 'Where is everybody? Have they all gone out?'

'Sure,' Lala told her, nodding solemnly. 'They're always out in the mornings. Why?' She studied Olivia with concern, her brown eyes huge. 'You feel lonely? Don't worry, I've got some English books. You can read to Greg, if you want.'

So Olivia spent the morning sitting in the blazing hot sunshine, reading to Greg from one of the very simple books Lala had given her. Greg was cheerful but restless, wanting to go into the village to see his friends. Olivia dissuaded him. She thought he would get too tired tramping about all over Solunto. He just wasn't well enough yet.

Nick had gone to Palermo, she discovered, with Tonino

to settle some business there. He apparently had some offices in the centre of the city.

In the afternoon she had to take a *siesta*. The *siesta* was religiously observed in Sicily, and Lala, Signora Baretta and Greg went off to bed when the sun reached its height.

Olivia was too restless. She wanted to walk down to the village but was rather apprehensive. She didn't know the way to begin with, and she didn't know any of the people there.

Nick and Tonino arrived back at seven. Olivia was in the kitchen with Lala, helping to prepare dinner, when they came in.

'Smells good,' commented Tonino, picking up a saucepan lid and peering into the pan, sniffing.

Lala smacked his hand. 'No peeping!' she told him, grinning. She put the lid back on the pan and asked, 'You have a good day?'

Tonino smiled, coming up behind her and sliding his hands round her waist. 'Not bad,' he said, and gave her a discreet kiss on the neck, his eyes smiling as he caught Olivia watching him.

Nick slid his hands into his pockets, looking at Olivia. 'How about you?' he asked, and his eyes held hers closely. 'What did you do?'

She shrugged. 'Nothing much.' She was apprehensive about telling him what she had really done. She had spent the morning with Greg in the garden, but the afternoon had been spent reading to him in his room.

Lala turned round with a bright smile. 'I gave her some books, to read to Gregorio. She looked after him all day.'

There was a little silence. Nick flicked his eyes back

to Olivia. 'Where?' he asked in a strangely neutral tone.

Olivia moistened her lips with her tongue tip. 'Here and there,' she said slowly.

Nick's face was stony. 'In his room?'

She felt her throat tighten. She nodded, her eyes intent on his face.

He looked at her, his mouth firming, then turned to Lala. 'Don't serve dinner for me,' he said tightly, 'I'm going out. I don't know when I'll be back.'

He turned, walking out of the kitchen without another word. Olivia stood totally still, listening to his footsteps echoing in the hall and then the slam of the front door followed by the powerful roar of an engine as his car pulled away from the house.

Tonino and Lala exchanged glances. Olivia bit her lip, looking at them out of the corner of her eye. Then she turned, putting on a calm face for their benefit.

'He's in a nasty mood!' she said brightly, her face flickering, uncertain as she looked at them. 'Has he been like this all day?'

'Sure,' Tonino said quietly, his eyes gentle. 'He'll feel better tomorrow.'

Olivia gave him a little smile. 'It must be working too hard,' she said, 'puts him in a bad temper!'

Tonino looked at her silently, his dark face wise.

She put the cloth she was holding on the table. 'I'll go and see how Greg is,' she said under her breath, and walked to the door in silence.

She was irritated with Nick for embarrassing her in front of Tonino and Lala like that. She had only spent the day with Greg because they had both been bored. There was nothing in it. She wasn't in love with him.

She had watched Greg carefully, and had seen with

relief that he had built up a fantasy around her. As far as she could see, he wasn't truly in love with her; he had just felt the pain of rejection too severely. It had been a case of rejection making her seem more desirable. She knew he would soon realise that for himself. But until then ... she sighed. She would just have to bide her time.

Nick didn't return until late that night. Olivia was in bed, and heard his footsteps on the corridor outside her room. She stiffened as he stopped for a moment outside her door. She held her breath, lying totally still. Then he moved away and she heard his door close quietly.

She jerked awake some time in the night. Lying still, she thought she heard Greg call out in the room next to hers. Fumbling for the light switch, she got out of bed and slipped her wrap on, jerking it tightly at her waist.

She went into the corridor, listening intently, then going towards Greg's room, she opened the door very quietly and went into the darkened room.

'Greg?' she whispered, listening in the darkness for sounds of movement. 'Are you all right?'

She heard him move restlessly on the bed. He was having a nightmare. She closed the door behind her and held her breath as it clicked shut far too noisily. Going over to the bed, she peered through the blackness at Greg's face.

'Sssh!' she whispered as he groaned in his sleep, turning over in the bed, the sheets rustling.

The door opened and Olivia froze. She saw Nick's shadow loom in the doorway and her heart plummeted in sudden fear.

His hand reached out to flick the light on. He took in

the scene at once—Olivia sitting frozen on the bed, staring at him in horror while Greg lay next to her.

Nick's face was dangerous. 'Get out of here!' he muttered under his breath, and Olivia stood up, swallowing.

He watched her, his body still, his chest gleaming bronze against the neck of his white towelling robe, his long legs visible where the robe ended, his hair-roughened thighs making Olivia's knees go weak with sudden sharp longing.

'He was having a nightmare,' she explained shakily as Nick closed the door behind her, flicking off the light.

He took her arm in a firm grip. 'Shut up,' he said bitingly then pushed her towards her own room and thrust her inside, closing the door behind him as he came in.

She backed away from him, seeing the fierce burning anger in his eyes. 'I heard him call out,' she said, swallowing.

'I didn't hear him,' said Nick between his teeth as he came towards her.

Olivia backed, her throat tight. 'Then how did you know I was in there?'

'I heard you moving about.' He was closer now, and Olivia felt herself begin to tremble, angry with herself for reacting like this. It was none of his business what she did.

'Oh,' she said, lost for words as her back touched the wall and she realised she was cornered.

'Yes, oh!' Nick said tightly, and his hands reached out, tangling in her hair, jerking her head back viciously. 'So much for your goddamned lies! "I don't want him, I don't want him!"' he mimicked, and Olivia flushed hotly. 'Like hell you don't want him!'

She looked at him with bitter resentment. 'He was having a nightmare!' she insisted, trying to pull herself away from him, but his hand tightened in her hair and she moaned in sudden pain.

'Come off it!' Nick's eyes burnt into hers. 'Do you think I'm stupid? You went in there to get your kicks!'

Olivia's breath caught in her throat at the insult. She stared at him bitterly, her eyes hating him. 'You're disgusting!' she said through her teeth. 'Don't you ever think of anything else?'

He gave a harsh crack of laughter. 'No, and neither do you. You're not content with one lover—you want us both!'

She stared at him in blazing, humiliating anger. 'You bastard,' she said in a low shaking voice, feeling her hands clench into tight fists at her sides.

'Does the truth sting?' he asked bitingly. 'I thought you were tougher than that. You've been running rings around both of us since I brought you back. Poor Greg!' he laughed. 'He thinks you're his. But we can both have you if we play along, can't we?'

Her hand flew out and slapped his cheek in blinding anger. His head jerked back and he stared down at her in blazing, violent fury, his eyes leaping with rage. Then his mouth clamped down on hers brutally, kissing her with ruthless fury until her lips bit back against her teeth, until she felt she could take no more. She struggled, trying to get away, but he was too strong, too insistent. She hit out at him with tightly balled fists, struggling, but he was more powerful and she couldn't move. Bitter anger flared inside her at his brutal treatment.

With one almighty effort she pushed him away,

breathing hard, her hands up against his shoulders.

'Do that again and I'll scream,' she said, watching him intently.

His mouth curled in a chilling smile. 'Scream,' he invited between his teeth. .

She saw him coming towards her again and took a deep breath, opening her mouth in a flare of panic. The loud piercing scream made him stop, staring at her incredulously.

The silence was deafening. Then she heard movements outside and stared at Nick. He was livid. His face was harsh with fury as he watched her, knowing there was nothing he could do.

The door opened, and Signora Baretta stood in her dressing gown, blinking against the light. She stared at them both in amazement, her eyes widening as she stood totally still.

'Damn you!' Nick bit out, throwing a furious look at Olivia before striding out of the room angrily, his lean body tense.

Signora Baretta just stared at Olivia. Then she recovered herself and asked slowly, 'Are you all right?'

Olivia nodded, feeling the hot colour flood her cheeks.

Signora Baretta watched her in silence for a moment, then nodded, closing the door without another word.

CHAPTER EIGHT

OLIVIA didn't see Nick for the next three days. She caught a glimpse of him in the evenings when he came in with Tonino, his eyes cold chips of ice as he looked at her. He would slam out of the house a moment later, going out to dinner with friends, and Olivia would sigh.

She spent her time helping Lala and Signora Baretta around the house. She sat with Greg occasionally, talking to him in the bright garden. The grass was slowly turning a bleached yellow as the sun grew stronger with each day. In the height of summer, parts of Sicily could become as hot as Africa. The sun turned everything on the land to dust with its heat.

Olivia spent one afternoon with Greg in the garden. He was restless after his *siesta*, fidgeting like a child waiting to be let out of school.

'I'm fed up with this place,' he complained, picking a leaf from a nearby tree and shredding it systematically with his fingers. 'Nick always orders me around. I don't see why I can't go out. I'm much better now, don't you think?'

'Of course, Greg,' she said, tongue in cheek. She smiled at him, her cheeks dimpling.

Greg laughed. 'I'll get you for that!' he said, coming towards her, his face bright under the sun's heat, his eyes twinkling.

Olivia backed, laughing. Then she stopped, as she saw

138

Simonetta coming towards them, looking startlingly beautiful in a white dress which clung to her voluptuous body.

Simonetta gave Greg a shy smile, her brown eyes shining. *'Ciao,'* she murmured, looking up at him.

'Hello,' said Greg, smiling down at her, his hands thrust into the pockets of his jeans. 'Are you bored too?'

'Never with you, Gregorio,' Simonetta said in a throaty voice. She took his hand, her olive-skinned face coaxing. 'Come for a walk,' she invited, looking at him through her thick lashes.

Olivia saw Greg's face change as he looked at her. 'Okay,' he said softly, and she wondered if he cared more for Simonetta than he thought he did. Greg began to walk away with the Sicilian girl, then turned, looking back at Olivia. 'Sorry!' he said, laughing. 'Do you want to come?'

Olivia's eyes met Simonetta's. 'No,' she said gently, and smiled, 'I'll go inside for a while.' Simonetta gave her a slow, grateful smile and walked away with Greg.

Olivia sighed, going back to the house. She wondered why Simonetta hadn't told Greg about the kiss she had seen. Perhaps she was sensible enough to realise it would all work out in the end.

When she came down to breakfast the next morning she had a shock to see Nick sitting at the table in the kitchen, reading a newspaper. He looked at her over the top of it with cool grey eyes.

'How are you?' he asked flatly.

Olivia gave him an uncertain smile. 'I'm fine,' she said huskily.

He watched her with steel grey eyes, then began reading again. She went over to the stove, her body tense, and poured herself a cup of coffee from the heavy metal coffee pot. Sitting down at the table, she kept her eyes on the floor, staying silent.

'I've got the day off,' Nick said suddenly, and she looked up in surprise, raising her brows.

'Oh,' she said, for want of anything else to say. She looked at the top of his black head behind the paper for a moment, wondering how she was supposed to reply.

Nick closed the paper with an irritable snap. 'I thought we might drive into Palermo,' he said tersely, and raised dark brows at her surprised look. 'Well?' he said irritably. 'Do you want to come or not?'

She nodded, spreading her hands in a shrug. 'Of course,' she began hesitantly, 'but . . .'

'Yes or no?' His voice was harsh, irritated.

Olivia felt her mouth compress. 'Yes,' she said under her breath, looking at him mutinously. He wasn't asking her out for the day, he was delivering an ultimatum.

'We'll leave in half an hour,' he said, his face brooding. He began to walk out of the kitchen, then looked down at her as he passed. 'And don't sulk!'

Olivia listened to his footsteps going down the hall and gritted her teeth. He was maddening, she decided, putting her cup down with a little crash. But at least he wasn't at her throat any more—just halfway to her throat, which was a compromise if nothing else.

Palermo was raucous and lively, filled with chattering lively people who walked along the narrow streets making as much noise as possible. They stood around market stalls and shops, gesturing wildly as they told each other the latest stories. Their faces were friendly and cheerful, their eyes following Olivia as she walked past with Nick.

The back streets were hung with washing, and a collection of women sat outside their houses talking to each other, nodding wisely and wagging fingers. They watched Olivia pass with interest, their eyes suspicious.

'Thirsty?' Nick asked as they walked into a huge piazza filled with fountains and statues.

Olivia nodded. 'Very,' she agreed, her eyes tracing with wonder the beauty of the enormous round-domed church that stood in the square. The fountains were in front of it, steps going down around it, and the sound of running water filled the warm air.

They stopped at a café at one side of the square and sat down in the open air. Nick lit a cigar, the smoke drifting from its dully glowing tip as he watched the people walking past.

'You like the statues?' he asked, following her gaze as she looked at the tall white stone figures of nude men and women in front of the church.

She smiled tentatively. 'They're beautiful,' she agreed, sipping her drink, feeling the cool liquid slide over her parched throat.

Nick laughed under his breath. 'The people didn't, when they were first unveiled. This place is known as the Piazza della Vergogna—the Square of Shame!' He shook his black head with a smile. 'Puritanic lot, some of the old ones.'

Olivia grinned, her cheeks dimpling, and looked back at the sculpted figures. No doubt the very proper Sicilians had been shocked on seeing the nude figures.

Nick was silent for a moment, watching her, oblivious to the noise of the people walking past chattering and gesturing noisily.

'Tell me about yourself,' he asked suddenly.

She looked round with a frown, seeing the hooded eyes which were unreadable. 'There's not much to tell,' she said slowly, shrugging. 'I'm twenty-three, I'm a model and I have one sister. My parents died when I was seventeen and I had to leave school and go out to work.' She shrugged again. 'I've been working ever since.' Her eyes met his in a brief silence. 'But then you know all that already, don't you?'

A smile curled his lips. 'I have my sources,' he agreed in a lazy drawl. Then he shrugged, gesturing with one long tanned hand. 'I just wanted to hear it from you.'

She raised her brows, a wry expression on her face. 'Why don't you look it up?' she said quietly. 'You must have a pretty big file on me.'

Nick's eyes narrowed. 'Very funny!' He sipped his cool drink, and looked away from her. 'A file can't tell me any more than a computer. I want to know about you,' his mouth compressed, 'and you're the only person who can tell me.'

She eyed him slowly. 'Do you mean men?'

He didn't laugh. He watched her with those deep grey eyes, silent for a long moment. Then he inclined his black head, studying her still. She felt a little unnerved.

'I haven't had many boy-friends,' she told him, her eyes screwing up against the glare of the sun. 'For a start, I don't really have time. But mainly, I've just never met anyone I've really fallen for.' She smiled. 'Unless you count infatuations.'

'No one special?' He was watching her intently.

She shook her head. 'No one,' she agreed quietly. She sipped her drink, resting her hand on the cool metal of the table they sat at. 'I was almost engaged once, though. But I broke it off because I knew I didn't really love him.'

There was a silence, and she sat quietly watching life passing by, the people around her noisy and boisterous. Shouts were heard from along the Pretoria, the whine of a motorcycle, the distant hooting of cars in the other streets.

'Love's very important to you?' Nick asked quietly.

She turned, studying him. 'Isn't it to you?'

He shrugged, his broad shoulders powerful beneath the crisp white shirt he wore. 'Of course,' he murmured, and his eyes slid to hers, hooded, unreadable. 'But it's very difficult to handle,' he watched her intently, 'isn't it?'

Olivia stared at him for a moment, trying to read the expression on his face. Then she bent her head, sipping her drink, evading his eyes.

He took her shopping at the end of the morning. They walked around the old quarter of the city, going into tourist shops, poking around among the different souvenirs which attracted Olivia.

She bought hundreds of presents for herself and her friends, all gaily wrapped. The shopkeepers exchanged indulgent looks with Nick and wrapped the presents in brightly coloured paper for her, handing them to her with nods and smiles.

'What do you want all this rubbish for?' Nick asked as he helped her carry the bright packages. He peered into one of the bags that was open. 'It's all junk!'

Olivia raised her brows. 'Look, whose money is it?' she asked, smiling, her arms laden with parcels of pottery and prettily dressed dolls. 'Besides, you live here. You're not likely to be interested in souvenirs.'

They began to walk back to the car which was parked in the back streets near the sea, quite close to La Cala.' Olivia looked up as they passed stone walls surrounding a park filled with flowers.

She sighed, closing her eyes as an exquisite scent drifted to her nostrils. 'How beautiful!' she exclaimed, looking in through the gates at the bright, dazzling array of tropical flowers, lush and fragrant.

'The Garibaldi Gardens,' Nick told her, following her gaze to the somewhat Oriental flowers. 'Someone once said that Palermo smells like a lady's bedroom.'

'A lady's bedroom?' ' Olivia repeated, raising her brows, smiling. 'And would you agree with that profound statement?'

Nick gave her a wicked, lazy smile. 'How should I know?' he drawled, eyes twinkling.

They walked back to the car, through the patched and peeling streets, hearing the noises of the city, mothers shouting to their children, the smell of cooking floating from the shuttered windows, the distant sound of traffic.

'How are you going to get all that lot back?' Nick asked, frowning quizzically as he put his load of parcels in the back of the car. 'You'll need a new suitcase.'

Olivia smiled, her cheeks dimpling. 'I'll pinch yours!' she said impishly.

He laughed, his head blotting out the glare of the sun as he looked down at her. 'Will you, indeed?' he muttered softly, and his hand reached out to stroke her chin. 'Be careful I don't catch you at it.'

She raised her brows in breathless challenge. 'What would you do?'

'This . . .' He bent his head, his lips brushing hers,

and her pulses leapt. He drew away, watching her intensely. 'Olivia ...' he began, but she broke away from him, confused.

'We'd better be getting back,' she said breathlessly, confused, flushing. His attitude was so different all of a sudden. She couldn't handle the sudden intensity in his eyes.

'I want to talk to you,' he said quietly, his hands on her shoulders.

'No!' Her voice was sharper than she meant it to be, her nerves tightening in consternation. 'I want to go back!' She felt hemmed in by the narrow dirty street.

'Don't push me away!' Nick's black brows were drawn in a frown as she held up a hand to prevent him coming nearer her.

Olivia's eyes darted and she got into the car, 'I'm fed up with being ordered around!' she said, slamming the front door of the car, feeling like a scalded cat.

'What the hell are you talking about?' he demanded angrily, jumping in beside her, his face harsh. 'I only want to talk to you!'

She looked at him for a brief moment, then turned, dumping her packages on the back seat and turning back to sit straight. She put her seat-belt on and waited for him to start the car. He didn't. He just sat, watching her with a heavy frown.

She looked at him. 'You think all you have to do is say the word,' she said in a low angry voice, aware that she was behaving irrationally, but unable to stop herself, 'but you've treated me too badly for that. Your trouble is, you've had everything too easy from the moment you were born.'

'Easy?' he said bitingly, and his face was suddenly

fiercely angry. He started the engine, revving it noisily. His foot pressed hard on the accelerator and they shrieked away, sending clouds of dust spilling and billowing at the wheels. 'You stupid little bitch! I've had to fight like an animal for everything I've got.'

Olivia's eyes flashed with temper. 'Don't give me that!' she looked at him angrily. 'Your home is worth a fortune! Your father stuck a silver spoon in your mouth at birth and it's still there!'

The tyres shrieked in protest as Nick screamed out of the city, his fingers tight on the steering wheel, showing white at the bone as he gripped it, his face carved from granite.

'My father,' he said through his teeth, 'disowned me when I was two. He left me and my mother to live in a hellhole in New York and ran off to Sicily to live it up with his mistresses.'

She looked at him, amazed. 'I don't believe you,' she said under her breath.

'I don't give a damn!' he snarled, bitterly angry. 'He came back on a whim when I was ten and stayed for six months. As soon as my mother was pregnant he scuttled back to Sicily.' His mouth tightened into a hard line,'My God, I hated him for that!'

She shook her head in disbelief. 'You mean he left knowing your mother was carrying Greg?'

He nodded, his face brooding as they sped across the wild terrain. He slammed the gear-stick into place, and she felt the power of the strong hand, saw the little network of black hairs curling over his wrist.

'She brought us both here when I was twelve,' his lips curled in a snarl at the memory, 'to show my father his child. He refused to see us.' Nick swore under his breath and said bitterly, 'The bastard! I stood in the garden, looking at the Palazzo Baretta and hating him. I wanted to kill him.'

Olivia bent her head, thoughts spinning through her mind. She had thought Nick had been given power, but she should have realised that no man's face could carry the stamp of ruthlessness, the stark uncompromising strength, unless he had fought grimly for his power.

'That house was my birthright,' Nick said under his breath, 'my blood right. And he was denying it to all of us. So I decided to take it from him.'

She looked at him slowly. 'How?'

His eyes were fierce as he looked at her. 'How the hell do you think? I fought my way to the top, and sat back, playing a waiting game. He was a fool. I knew he'd spend all his money eventually. As soon as he was bankrupt I stepped in.'

'What did you do?' Olivia asked, holding her breath, fascinated by the story.

Nick laughed, and her blood ran cold. 'I made him an offer he couldn't refuse!' His head swung to look at her briefly, and he smiled, his lips chilling. 'Then I chucked him out, with pleasure.' He was silent for a moment, then said, 'He wasn't a father to me. I wanted to break his damned neck, but my mother wouldn't let me.'

Olivia bent her head. She had misjudged him. She raised her eyes slowly, swallowing on a tight throat, her eyes ashamed as she looked at his harsh face.

'I'm sorry,' she said quietly, and laid a tentative hand on his arm.

He didn't even look at her. 'Shut up,' he said bitingly, and let her hand fall from his arm as they screeched around narrow bends towards Solunto.

When they got back to the house, Nick strode straight in without looking at her. Olivia sighed, feeling the tension slowly ease from her body as she watched him go.

She had offended him, she realised, sighing. She decided to take a walk down to the village. It shouldn't be too far, and she wanted time to think, time to remember everything Nick had said.

As she walked down the hill she saw three youths coming towards her.

'Ecco!' one of them said, his olive-skinned face admiring as he looked at her. *'Bella, no?'* he nudged his friends, who grinned, nodding, coming towards her.

Olivia smiled politely. *'Scusi,'* she said, trying to move past. They laughed, pushing her back and stepping in her way. The yellowed grass moved in the breeze, the insects whined around her. The three youths licked their lips in admiration, running their eyes over her.

Olivia felt suddenly uneasy. Their eyes were eating her as though she was a strange new delicacy. She saw the looks on their faces as they edged closer and swallowed, her throat tight.

'Go away!' she said, lapsing into English in her fright.

They laughed, exchanging knowing looks. One of them reached out, running his hand over her hair, and Olivia brushed his hand away sharply, her face worried and tense, her heart beating faster, her face losing its colour.

'Basta!' Nick's voice cracked like a whip into the sinister afternoon.

The youths looked up quickly, and paled, their faces filling with sudden fear. They backed, sliding their caps off in a gesture of respect. Their eyes were nervous, frightened.

'Signore Baretta,' one of them said, swallowing nervously.

Olivia turned her head slowly. Nick was standing watching with narrowed eyes, his tall lean body tense. Tonino was with him, his dark face solemn.

Nick walked slowly with animal threat in his body, his narrowed dangerous eyes fixed on the three youths. He came to stand by Olivia, looking down at her in the tense, threatening silence.

'Go back to the house,' he told her in a chilling voice, and raised one hand, crooking one long finger. Tonino stepped forward instantly. 'Walk with her,' he told Tonino.

Olivia hesitated, then began to walk over to Tonino.

Nick turned back to the three youths, who were now stammering nervously, beginning to sweat as they feverishly tried to explain to him.

Olivia walked back up the hill with Tonino. 'Who were they?' she asked him as they walked.

Tonino shrugged. 'Just some boys from the village,' he told her, sliding his hands into the pockets of his double-breasted suit.

She frowned, looking over her shoulder as they turned the corner. 'What were they saying to Nick?' she asked, looking back at Tonino. 'And why were they so frightened?'

Tonino shrugged again, his feet kicking gently at the dusty road. 'They said they did not know who you were.'

Olivia frowned. She gave him an uncertain smile and raised her brows. 'Who am I?'

Tonino looked at her for a moment in silence. Then he said, 'They said they did not know you were Nick Baretta's girl.'

Her mouth opened in amazement. She shut it again, staring at Tonino, her footsteps halting until she stood totally still, her eyes widening. Nick Baretta's girl? The words burnt into her, branding her as she felt her heart start to thud faster.

'But,' she laid a hand on Tonino's arm, feeling the soft dark sleeve beneath her fingertips, 'Tonino . . . I'm not his girl!'

Tonino looked at her with those dark, wise eyes. 'You better tell Nick, not me,' he said quietly.

Olivia was tense when she reached the house. Tonino's words were spinning in her mind, fluttering like moths as they beat against her brain until her thoughts became incoherent, muddled, confused.

She went into the kitchen, following Tonino, her head bent, a frown marring her brow. She barely heard Lala speak to her; she was too preoccupied with everything that had happened. The look on Nick's face when he arrived to see her being accosted by those youths had been frightening.

The sinister silence which had fallen at Nick's appearance had been unnerving. She had felt a strange sense of elation at the same time, and that worried her more than she cared to admit to herself. And then Tonino's words afterwards . . . Nick Baretta's girl.

She almost felt the words brand into her flesh, white-hot in their intensity, and her eyes closed for a brief moment, trying to regain control as her heart began to hammer strangely inside her. Perhaps it's because I want to be known as Nick Baretta's girl, she thought with a jolt of sharp panic. Perhaps I want to see that almost dangerously possessive look on his face when I'm talking to another man.

She shook her head, trying to clear it. Lala was talking to

her, and she knew she could hardly understand the words she was saying. They were floating over her head, and she brought herself back to reality as best she could.

'They touched you?' Lala asked in an incredulous whisper. She looked at Tonino, her eyes wide. 'I don't believe it!'

Tonino nodded solemnly. 'No, really,' he said with total sincerity, 'is true. They stroked her hair, just as I walked up with Nick.'

The slam of the front door made Olivia jump nervously. She looked towards the door in tense anticipation as she heard Nick's footsteps approach the kitchen, and the turn of the doorhandle.

The door opened, and Nick stood watching them. There was a brief tense silence. Olivia slowly raised her eyes to his face and her eyes widened as she did so.

A dark bruise stained his angular cheekbone, just below his eye, giving him an even more dangerous appearance, making him look even more tough. She swallowed, her hands linking unsteadily in her lap.

Tonino and Lala looked at each other slowly. 'See you later,' they muttered, and walked out of the room, making a careful path around Nick, their eyes fixed on his bruised cheek.

The silence was almost tangible. Olivia moistened her lips with her tongue and asked, 'How did you get that?' looking at his bruise.

He ran one long tanned finger over his cheek. 'One of them was brave,' he drawled, and the grey eyes flicked to her. She noticed his knuckles were grazed. 'But don't worry, they won't be doing any flirting for quite some time.'

Olivia felt a thump of exhilarated pride. There was

something almost primordial in knowing that Nick had defended her, had used physical violence on her behalf. He had obviously taken all three of them on, and come out with only one bruise. Not bad going, she thought, feeling the thud of her heart.

A deep emotional charge ran through her as she thought of it. The animal violence in him was both exciting and frightening. She looked at the bruise on his hard face and felt her pulses quicken.

Nick came to stand in front of her and she tried desperately to push her confused feelings aside as she watched him towering over her.

'Why did you do it?' he asked flatly.

She raised her eyes to his. 'I didn't know I'd be attacked,' she pointed out, her face calm. But she wanted to stand up and cheer, throw roses and applaud him for sorting out those youths on her behalf. 'I just wanted to go for a walk to the village.'

His mouth compressed. 'A walk?' he repeated in a strangely tense voice. He looked down at her with an unreadable expression. 'Would you walk on your own in a deserted street in London? Or in New York?'

She frowned, feeling uneasy all of a sudden. 'That's different,' she said slowly. She moistened her lips with her tongue tip, and Nick's eyes followed the little movement intensely. 'I thought I'd be safe in open countryside.'

One hand snaked out to take her chin, thrusting her head back. He looked down into her eyes, his face hard. 'You don't understand the people here, do you?' he said, and the long fingers began to hurt her. 'But most of all you don't understand the men.'

She tried to draw away, but his hand held her still. 'Look,' she said in sudden confusion, 'men are men, wherever they're from.' She tried to stand up, but Nick's hand forced her to sit down again, and she looked at him angrily. 'Don't push me around!'

He raised one dark brow. She tried to stand up again, but his hand flew to her chest and he pushed her back.

'I've noticed one thing,' she said angrily, pushing at the hand which still lay at the top of her breasts, 'Sicilian men are a lot more violent than any others!'

Nick gave her tight smile. 'You're right,' he drawled tightly, 'they are a lot more violent. Especially where their women are concerned.'

She looked at him in silence, her eyes tracing the aggressive line of cheek and jaw, the vivid angry bruise on his cheek where he had no doubt punched the hell out of those men. She thought of his lean body, his strong hands as he threw punches, and shivered.

Nick was watching her. 'Haven't you ever heard of the Sicilian Vespers? The incident which triggered off a war?'

Olivia shook her head slowly.

'In the thirteenth century,' he told her, his fingers sliding to her neck, 'a French officer insulted a young Sicilian bride on her way to church.' His eyes darkened as though it was an inherent part of his memory. 'The people reacted violently.'

Her eyes were intent on his face, and she frowned. 'What did they do?' she asked slowly.

His gaze held hers. 'They massacred an entire French garrison.'

She swallowed, her throat tight. 'What does that have to do with me?' she asked.

Nick's black head tilted to one side as he studied her. 'It should point something out to you. Here, English girls are looked on as another breed. Sicilian girls are for marrying, but English girls are another matter entirely.'

She heard the words like a physical blow. She suddenly felt sick, looking at him through a mist of anger and humiliation. He couldn't have been more specific if he'd tried.

'I see!' She stood up angrily, her eyes a bright blue, her face tight. 'That's how you think of me, is it? No wonder you didn't want me to marry Greg!' She laughed bitterly. 'I'm not good enough for your precious brother, am I?'

His face hardened. 'You know damned well that wasn't what I meant!' he said harshly.

'Wasn't it?' She faced him, and her blue eyes flashed with temper. 'What did you mean, then? That you don't think the same way? Come on! Do you think I'm stupid?'

Nick's mouth firmed into an angry line. He looked about to say something, then stopped, running a hand through his thick black hair, watching her with harsh temper evident in every line of his face.

'You can't walk round unaccompanied,' he said tightly. 'Take someone with you next time.'

'There won't be a next time,' she said in a low voice, 'because I'm getting off this wretched island the next chance I get!'

There was a stunned silence, then Nick's eyes flashed and his hands went to her shoulders, the long fingers biting into them. He stared down at her, his face grim.

'You don't mean that!'

'Oh yes, I do!' she retorted, and tried to pull herself out of his grasp, but he jerked her back. 'I'm sick of you and your family!'

His hand moved to the back of her head, thrusting into her black hair, holding her head still. 'If you go,' he muttered between tightly clenched teeth, 'I'll follow. I'll be behind you every step of the way.'

Olivia shivered with alarm. He meant it. Her whole body was as taut as a bowstring. 'I don't care if you follow me to the moon and back,' she said under her breath.

His eyes were burning into her intensely. 'I would,' he said in a raw dangerous voice, and Olivia felt her heart stop for one incredulous moment before kicking back into life with a power that frightened her. 'I'd follow you to hell.'

Their eyes met and fused, and Olivia felt herself start to tremble, her pulses quickening like lightning, her heart thudding heavily against her breastbone.

She swallowed, her throat tightening. Her hands clung to his shoulders in fear that she might overbalance.

'Let go of me!' she whispered in overwhelming, breathless panic.

Nick's gaze burnt on her mouth for a breathtaking second, then he slowly raised the grey, smoky eyes to hers. She felt the long fingertips bite into her skin.

'Olivia . . .' he said deeply, his voice thickening.

Then the door opened, and a stunned silence that was almost tangible fell over them. They turned their heads, looking slowly towards the doorway, and Olivia felt her heart nosedive.

Greg looked from one to the other of them in incredulous shock. 'What the hell is going on?' he muttered under his breath.

CHAPTER NINE

OLIVIA looked at Greg with pain-filled eyes. The silence seemed to beat into her, her heart thudding out a slow rhythm reminding her of a death march. The expression on his face was one of bewilderment. He didn't understand what had been going on, he had no inkling of the deep feelings which had blown up between Nick and Olivia since their first meeting.

Olivia couldn't face it. She pushed past Greg, running up the hall and up the stairs to her bedroom. She locked the door and leaned against it, her forehead creased with pain.

She should have told Greg a long time ago that she wasn't going to marry him. Now he had no doubt found out—the hard way. She sighed, walking over to the bed and sitting down heavily.

She raged silently inside at Nick. He had offended her deeply, hurt her, she now realised. His words had made her feel physically sick when he said English girls were another breed. He obviously held the same view as the other men.

Sicilian girls are for marrying, she thought bitterly, English girls are just for fun.

Why should that worry me? she thought dismally. But she knew. She had fallen in love with him somehow. She felt the hot tears prick the back of her lids and gritted her teeth.

Somewhere along the line, he had touched a chord

deep inside her, and that touch had grown until she was filled with him. She had thought at first that there was nothing more than physical attraction between them— he was a devastatingly attractive man, after all. But she hadn't realised how strong the attraction was.

Until it had exploded, blown up in her face. The sexual power between them was shattering. But it was only shattering because there were deeper feelings behind it.

No kiss could make them both feel like that unless there was deep emotion in it. She bit her knuckles in an effort to keep control. It's your own stupid fault, she told herself. You should never have let him near you. It was the physical contact that had fed the seed of their attraction.

Perhaps he was going through the same hell that she was. Her eyes flicked open, widening in a sudden flare of hope. But she sighed bitterly, realising that Nick only wanted to go to bed with her. He had made that clear from the start. I want to fall into your bed, not your heart, he had said, and she knew he meant it. He wasn't in love with her. He just wanted to make love to her.

A knock on the door brought her head up and she stiffened, wiping her eyes with a trembling hand.

'Who is it?' she asked in a pretence of composure.

There was a pause, then: 'Greg.'

Her shoulders sagged. She had thought it was Nick. 'Come in,' she said with a sigh. She would have to face him sooner or later. Better to get it over with now.

Greg opened the door slowly, and stared at her, seeing the redness of her eyes. 'The swine!' he muttered under his breath, and took a step towards the bed. 'He hurt you. I'm sorry, Olivia, I'll make sure it doesn't happen again.'

She eyed him sadly. Nick hadn't told him. 'Sit down, Greg,' she said quietly.

He watched her for a moment, then came towards the bed, sitting down slowly next to her. His body was still as he watched her, as though he half guessed what was on her mind.

She took a deep breath and said quietly, 'I'm not going to marry you, Greg.'

He sat totally still for a second, then asked deeply, 'Why?' His eyes searched her face. 'Is it because of Nick? Did he tell you not to marry me? I know the way he thinks, Olivia, I know the way . . .'

'No,' she said firmly, 'it's nothing to do with Nick.' She linked her hands in her lap, and said, 'I never intended to marry you. I just went along with it because I was frightened of what you might do.'

'I see,' he said stiffly.

She was handling this badly, she knew, and she laid a hand over his. 'I wanted to tell you before, but,' she sighed, 'I just didn't have the guts, I suppose. Everytime I tried to tell you, the words came out wrong.'

'So you let me go on believing it,' he said bitterly, and Olivia flushed feeling a complete bitch.

'I'm sorry, Greg,' she said under her breath, bending her head. She felt inadequate. She tried to think of something else to say, but her mind drew a blank.

Greg sighed heavily, and rested his head in his hands. 'No,' he said, 'I'm the one who should apologise. I had no right to try emotional blackmail on you the way I did.' His fists clenched and he muttered, 'I acted like a spoiled child.' He looked across at her. 'I'm sorry. I can't understand what got into me.'

Olivia squeezed his hand without speaking, giving him a brief smile.

There was a brief silence, then Greg asked, 'So what happens now?' He studied her face with a frown. 'Are you going to leave? Or is there something else to keep you here?'

She looked up sharply, and felt the hot colour flood her face as she met his gaze. 'I don't know,' she answered, shrugging as she looked away. 'I haven't given it much thought, to tell the truth.'

'Maybe you should talk it over with Nick,' he said with a trace of bitterness, and Olivia winced inside.

She raised her head slowly and studied his face for a moment. 'Simonetta told you,' she said under her breath.

Greg hesitated, then he sighed. 'Yes.'

She ought to have realised. She had thought Simonetta wouldn't tell anyone about her kissing Nick in the garden. But of course she had told Greg. She was in love with him, after all. Olivia suddenly wished she had never met Nick, never laid eyes on him. Then she dug her nails in her palm and frowned. How empty my life would have been, she thought, and a bitter smile touched her lips. Without Nick the world seemed un-liveable in somehow. But being with him, and knowing he didn't love her, was almost too painful for her.

'Olivia?' Greg was looking at her anxiously, his eyes concerned. 'I was talking to you.'

'Sorry,' she looked up with a pretence of a smile, 'I was miles away.'

Greg studied her clearly. 'You're in love with him, aren't you?' he said quietly.

She felt tears prick the back of her eyes, her throat

began to sting. 'Yes,' she said, bending her head.

He sighed, watching her. Then he slid his arms round her, holding her close to him while she turned her face into his chest. 'You silly little idiot,' he said gently, his hands comforting as he stroked her hair.

A halting footfall in the doorway made Olivia stiffen. She felt Greg move, turning his head, and the hair on the back of her neck prickled with unease. She slowly raised her head to look over his shoulder.

Nick stood in the doorway, his features hard. 'Have fun!' he said bitingly, and his eyes flashed before he turned on his heel and strode angrily down the corridor, his footsteps ringing out with a menacing clarity that made her want to cry out loud.

Olivia's eyes closed in disbelief. It was just too unfair of him to come in at that moment! She listened, her face rigid, as the ferocious engine of the car roared and snarled viciously as it screamed away down the drive.

Olivia was up early the next day. The sun had woken her up, stroking her eyelids with lazy golden fingers. She went downstairs quickly, reaching the hallway just as the kitchen door opened and Nick came striding out.

She looked at him uncertainly. 'Good morning.' Her eyes scanned his face.

'You're up early,' he drawled in an icy voice, and his eyes flicked over her coldly. 'Planning an outing?'

She paled at the tone of his voice. 'I don't know,' she said quietly, 'I might go out later.'

His smile was tight. 'With Greg, of course.'

She bent her head, biting her lip. He was being very unfair. 'I'd have to ask Greg,' she agreed, running a hand through her hair and watching him with troubled eyes. 'He might not want to go out.'

'I'm sure you can accommodate him,' he said, and his voice sniped at her. 'You cater to his needs very well. If he wants you in his room, you go. If he wants you in the garden, you go.' His lips curled in a sneer. 'The perfect wife for him!'

She felt her mouth begin to tremble at the unpleasant words, and raised her head angrily. 'Jealous, Nick?' she asked before she could stop herself.

His eyes leapt with rage. 'You little bitch!' he bit out through his teeth, and his hands clenched into fists at his sides. He looked about to speak, but at that moment there was movement from outside.

'Boss!' Tonino pushed the front doors open, the sunlight haloed around his dark head. His eyes flicked from Olivia to Nick and he stood silently, watching, his dark figure tall in the doorway.

Nick's eyes narrowed. 'What is it?'

Tonino hesitated, the dark eyes moving slowly to Olivia's face. He slid his hands in his pockets, his double-breasted suit enhancing his stylish appearance.

'Signor Scaletta just drove in through the gates,' he told Nick, his eyes moving back to him.

Nick's eyes narrowed and a sudden tension filled his lean body. 'Scaletta,' he said under his breath, and his face hardened. 'What the hell does he want?'

Olivia frowned, tilting her head to one side. Outside came the sound of car doors slamming, the tread of feet on the dusty driveway, smooth Italian voice talking in the hot morning as they approached the house.

'Signore Baretta!' A man appeared in the doorway, his voice soft and insipid as he spoke. Olivia shivered as she looked at him.

Scaletta's eyes were flat, lifeless. A cold black, they reminded her of the eyes of a dead fish staring up from a slab. His hair was black, slicked back from his olive-skinned swarthy face. He wore a superbly cut grey suit.

Nick took a step towards him. 'What do you want, Scaletta?' he asked in a dangerously soft voice.

Scaletta smiled and a shudder went through Olivia. 'We are old friends,' he said in that soft voice. 'Why should I not drop in to see you from time to time?'

Nick's eyes were icy. 'You're not welcome here, Scaletta,' he said, and the menace in his voice was frightening.

Scaletta looked at Olivia, and raised his brows. 'Beautiful,' he said under his breath, watching her shiver with distaste. He took a step forwards.

'Get away from her,' ordered Nick in a sinister undertone.

Scaletta smiled again, and his eyes moved slowly back to Olivia. 'You must forgive him,' he said, his soft voice sending icy shudders down her spine. 'He is too Sicilian—too hot-blooded.' The dead black eyes ran over her with deliberation. 'But you must know that already.'

She took an involuntary step back as he moved towards her. There was something cold-blooded about him, something inherently nasty that made her feel physically ill.

Nick stepped forwards immediately, blocking his path. 'Get out of here,' he said in a quiet but menacing tone.

Their eyes met for a long moment, and Scaletta was the first to look away. Only a fool would mistake the sinister, deadly expression on Nick's face.

Scaletta shrugged, conceding the point. 'I have a business proposition for you, my friend,' he said a moment later. 'It might interest you.' He smiled and Olivia felt her flesh crawl. 'It might interest you very much indeed.'

'I doubt it,' Nick said smokily

Scaletta's smile was slow. 'Don't be too quick to decide,' he told him.

Nick's eyes narrowed. He turned to Olivia and said, 'Go into the other room.' When she didn't move he said, 'Go on,' and watched her intently until she moved away from him, walking into the kitchen with a worried face.

About ten minutes later she heard Nick's car pull away down the drive followed quickly by another car, no doubt Scaletta's. She shivered as she remembered him. He had to be the most unlikeable person she had ever laid eyes on. She had disliked him on sight.

She spent the day thinking about Nick while she worked around the house with Lala. He had been so angry when she first came downstairs, but his anger had soon turned to menacing aggression when Scaletta appeared. She asked Lala about him, curious to know who he was.

Lala just looked at her strangely and said, 'You must ask Nick that.' Her voice was quiet as she spoke. 'It is not for me to answer.'

So Olivia dismissed the man from her mind. It wasn't difficult. Nick was constantly in her thoughts, disturbing her sleep when she took a *siesta* in the afternoon. He was in her bloodstream, and just the thought of him made her pulses leap.

Nick and Tonino came in later than usual. He looked

at her as she passed him in the hall, and her heart began to thud inside her for that brief moment. Then he flicked his gaze away brusquely, and went upstairs to change into a dinner suit. Olivia went back to the kitchen to help Lala, her eyes sad.

She paled as the kitchen door opened and Nick came in.

'I'll be back around midnight,' he said in a cool voice without looking at Olivia, 'so don't hold dinner for me.'

Lala nodded. 'Sure,' she said quietly.

Nick adjusted his cufflink, the gold glinting like sunlight against the black material of his jacket, the white of his cuff. Olivia's heart thudded like a steam hammer. She was scared by her loss of control.

Nick turned to her, his eyes avoiding hers. 'Have you set the date for the party yet?' he asked, and she was unable to reply. The words stuck in her throat. Tonino and Lala were watching, her nerves were jumping, and she didn't seem able to tell him in front of them. She felt a sudden rush of desperation, her eyes darting back to Nick, and laid a hand on the table to steady herself.

Her eyes ran over him with sudden sharp longing. He looked devastatingly attractive in the impeccably cut black dinner suit. She wanted to reach out and run her fingertips over his broad shoulders. She bit her lip, holding herself steady. It was now or never.

She took a deep breath. 'We're not having an engagement party.'

Nick's eyes flicked to hers immediately. 'What?' His face was intense as he stared at her.

'No,' Olivia fumbled for the words, her heart beating rapidly. She was suddenly overcome with nerves as she faced that intent, burning gaze. 'We decided against it in the end.'

'When was this?' His voice was urgent.

She swallowed. 'Last night, yesterday. We had a long talk together and finally agreed . . .'

'Yes,' Nick cut in, his tone hardening, 'I saw your little talk.' His eyes held biting contempt. He thrust his hands in his pockets and looked at Tonino and Lala, who were watching, their silence sympathetic. Nick's mouth hardened. 'Goodnight!' he muttered, turning on his heel and leaving without another word.

Olivia slammed her hand hard against the wall. 'Damn!' she muttered under her breath.

She went to bed early, unable to sit around any more because her thoughts were too painful. But changing rooms didn't help. The pain didn't go away, neither did the thoughts. They whirred and jabbed at her as she lay on her bed, tossing and turning.

Dinner had been grey for Olivia. She had sat quietly at the table, her eyes down, her lashes sweeping her cheeks as she listened to the rest of the family talking.

Greg had been in high spirits. He had taken Simonetta to the Roman ruins just over the hill, on the slopes of Monte Catalfano. He enthused about the day, his arms waving around as he searched for superlatives with which to describe how enjoyable it had been.

After dinner Olivia managed to get him on his own for a few moments to ask him about Scaletta. Greg had been reluctant to tell her, but in the end he gave way.

'Scaletta's mother was one of my father's mistresses,' he told Olivia, and nodded as he saw her shocked expression. 'He and Nick are arch-enemies. Scaletta tried to buy this house at the same time as Nick stepped in.'

He shrugged, giving her a little grin. 'Scaletta doesn't like losing, but as Nick said, that's just his tough luck.'

Olivia thought of that conversation now as she lay in bed. What chance did she have with someone like Nick? He was cynical, his attitude shaped by years of bitter struggling, grimly clawing his way to the top.

He had women coming out of his ears. They broke a leg to get to him first, fighting each other for his favours. Where did he go night after night if not to a woman? She suddenly felt physically sick at the thought of it, her stomach clenching, her throat constricting.

She didn't do much sleeping after that. Her mind was too full, too ready to think of Nick. She couldn't get to sleep however hard she tried.

At two o'clock in the morning she finally gave up. Pointless, she told herself, getting out of bed and slipping her wrap on. She tiptoed out of the room, closing the door gently behind her. Looking towards Nick's room, she saw it was in darkness. At least someone can sleep, she thought bitterly. His night isn't disturbed the way mine is.

The stairs creaked, deliberately it seemed, as she carefully went down them. Even you're against me, she thought, looking at them irritably. They creaked back in response as she got to the bottom of the stairs.

A light was on. She frowned, peering at the bottom of the door where light spilled out of the main room. Signora Baretta? she thought, going towards the door, her hand reaching hesitantly for the handle.

She pushed the door open. It creaked a little in protest. Her eyes blinked against the light and she felt her mouth open in shock as she saw who was there.

Nick looked round, his face haggard. 'Who is it?' he

snapped, then his eyes met hers.

'Nick . . .' Olivia whispered, astonished as she looked at him.

His jacket was off, his waistcoat undone, his shirt unbuttoned at the neck. His long legs rested on the floor, outstretched as though he was worn out. A bottle of whisky was in one hand, a glass in the other.

'What the hell do you want?' he asked in an angry mutter. The bottle tilted, the whisky spilling out into his glass, the harsh sound of glass hitting glass reaching her ears.

Olivia moistened her lips with her tongue, staring at him. 'I couldn't sleep,' she said quietly.

His lips curled. 'Lonely, were you?' he drawled, and raised the glass to his lips. He drank a little, then his eyes met hers above the rim of the glass. 'Enjoying the show?' he asked tightly.

Olivia swallowed. 'I think I'd better go back to bed,' she said under her breath, and turned to walk out of the room, aware that he was in a bad temper.

She heard the crash as he stood up, knocking the table over, the whisky bottle thudding on the floor, whisky spilling out on the carpet, and looked over her shoulder in sudden alarm.

Nick shook his black head. 'Now look what you've made me do,' he drawled, and his eyes narrowed on her. 'I shall have to think of something else to put me to sleep.'

Olivia swallowed, her pulses quickening. She eyed him warily. 'Why don't you have a glass of milk?' she said in sudden nervous humour, and immediately wished she hadn't said it.

He smiled, and she felt her blood turn to ice. 'A little

too tame for my present mood,' he drawled. 'What I need is something to knock me out, stone cold.' His gaze swept slowly over her, and she felt her heart thud faster. 'You're very good at that, aren't you?'

She clung to the door, her eyes wide. 'I gave him sleeping pills,' she said, her voice strained.

'What's your prescription for me?' he asked in a disturbing voice, and raised one brow, coming towards her, his lean body tense.

She felt her knees weaken. 'Nick——,' she began, backing away, but her back was up against the wall and he was standing in front of her now, towering over her.

'Something to ease the tension,' Nick drawled tightly, and his hand reached out to tangle in her hair, the long fingers stroking the nape of her neck while she stared at him. 'Something to make me feel calm, something to make me forget.'

Hope flickered inside her and she swallowed. 'Forget what?' she asked breathlessly.

He smiled tightly. 'To forget . . .' and his hands moved round her throat, slowly encircling it, 'how much I'd like to kill you.' His eyes glittered down into hers. 'What do you suggest?'

Olivia didn't reply. She just stood there, staring up at him, torn between running away from him in fear or sliding her arms around his neck and kissing him.

'No ideas?' he drawled, raising one brow. 'Never mind,' he smiled tightly. 'I've just had an inspiration,' and his eyes dropped to the neck of her wrap, focussing on the gleaming white of her breasts, heaving with emotion while he watched.

His hand moved slowly to her waist, and one long finger slid into the belt holding the wrap together. Then he pulled it, tugging on it until it fell apart and he could see her body outlined beneath the sheer nightdress.

He stared at her intently, his eyes burning on her body. 'Very pretty,' he drawled, his voice slurring. He reached out one hand. It fell heavily on her breast, and his breathing quickened.

He raised his eyes to hers. There was a long intense silence. All she could hear was the drumming of her heart.

'Dear God,' Nick said thickly, and his eyes closed for a moment. She watched a muscle begin to jerk rapidly in his cheek.

'Nick?' She looked at him anxiously, and laid a hand on his chest. The violent crash of his heart made her body begin to shake, her fingertips trembling on his chest.

His lids flicked open and their eyes fused with a jolt. 'Don't you understand?' he said between his teeth, and then his hands tightened on her, his face darkening intensely. 'Olivia,' he said in a hoarse, strangled voice.

His arms slid round her tightly, his hot mouth taking hers while he crushed her against him, moulding her to the hard length of his body. Her arms slid round his neck, tangling her fingers in his hair as she kissed him back with a flare of hunger.

His mouth moved urgently on hers as the kiss deepened. Fire licked through them as they pressed together with an urgency that was breathtaking, making the blood pound in her ears. She clung to him as the liquid heat flooded through her.

Nick raised his head, his breathing ragged. 'You're driving me out of my mind,' he said thickly, his teeth clamped together. His eyes fell on her breasts and a low animal moan came from his throat.

His hands shook as he touched her, then he ripped the soft delicate front of her nightdress. His hand slid over her breast and he stared fixedly at it. Then his mouth came back to hers, his hands sliding sensually over her body, branding her with a white-hot intensity that made her knees buckle. His mouth slid hotly to her throat, his teeth biting gently at her skin while she shivered, her eyes closed, stroking his head with shaking hands.

His tongue snaked out across her nipple and she moaned from deep in her throat, her heart hammering. His mouth moved hungrily back to hers, kissing her until she almost lost her mind.

'Does he make you feel like this?' he asked thickly, kissing her until her knees buckled. 'My brother?' His hands ran urgently over her body, and his breathing was ragged. 'Does he make you tremble?'

Olivia shook her head, her mind drugged and clouded. 'No,' she moaned, arching towards him as his hands slid to her thighs.

'Does he make you ache every time you look at him?' he asked in a raw, strangled voice, his lips driving her crazy as they kissed her throat. 'Does it hurt when he looks away from you?'

Her eyes flicked open, her body tightening. 'No,' she said in a tight whisper, her hands stiffening on his hair as alarm ran through her.

Nick raised his head, fire leaping from his eyes. 'Then why the hell are you going to marry him?' he shouted. Then he thrust her away from him and wrenched open the door violently.

'Nick!' she stumbled as she tried to follow him, holding her nightdress together, her mouth swollen from his kisses.

But he had gone by the time she was in the hall. The front door was swinging open, and she ran to it, heaving the great oak door back, her eyes wide, her face chalk white.

'Nick!' she whispered in a sob as she watched the tail lights of his car blaze into the night, the engine roaring.

The breeze rippled against her sheer nightdress as she clutched the ripped bodice to her shivering breasts. She clung to the doorhandle, her knuckles white. Tears blurred her vision, her heart wrenching. It hurt to watch him drive away from her. Hot salty tears flowed over her cheeks to her mouth, trickling down her pale alabaster skin while she stood in the doorway, staring into the night, wishing she could bring him back.

She overslept. The night had been disturbed, filled with restless images of his face, and it wasn't until five in the morning that she fell asleep. She scrambled out of bed the minute she opened her eyes, hurrying to get dressed before going downstairs, hoping she would see Nick.

Tonino was whistling when she walked into the kitchen. 'Good morning,' he said with a wide grin, his slim hands deftly arranging a bunch of bright pink flowers in a vase.

Olivia gave him a smile, acting casually as she said, 'Have you seen Nick?'

Tonino's hands stilled. 'Oh. Nick.' He watched her for a second, then his long elegant fingers began to briskly arrange the flowers again. 'Nick's gone to Siracusa.'

She watched him, biting her lip as she tried to place

the name. 'Siracusa? But that's on the other side of the island, isn't it?' Her eyes widened slowly and she said, 'He hasn't gone to see that man, has he?'

Tonino looked perplexed for a moment, then said, 'No!' forcefully, and shook his head. 'You crazy? Nick wouldn't have anything to do with Scaletta if you held a shotgun to his head!'

Olivia relaxed, then walked out of the kitchen, lost once more in her thoughts. She was very glad that Nick would have nothing to do with Scaletta. She had disliked him on sight, and every time she thought of him the dislike grew more intense.

She spent the day like any other. The afternoon sun forced her inside to take a restless siesta, escaping the blazing heat for a few hours. It wasn't until the early evening that she ventured outside again.

The garden was tranquil when she went out, the atmosphere almost melodic in its peacefulness. She was too bored and restless to sit inside, her thoughts constantly turning to Nick, brooding over every word he had said to her the previous night, every expression on his face. She relived again and again the moments when he had kissed her, feeling the thudding of her heart with a slightly breathless smile.

'Mind if I join you?' Greg's voice brought her out of her thoughts as his shadow fell across the lawn. She smiled, moving up so he could share her idyllic seat beneath the lush green trees. He sat quickly beside her, stretching his long jean-clad legs out before him. 'It makes me feel so lazy,' he murmured after a few seconds. They sat in silence in the warm evening tranquility, listening to the insects buzzing and dancing, the somnolent atmosphere somehow draining.

Greg picked a blade of yellowed grass and began chewing on it, twisting it around in his mouth. 'All I need now are gumboots!' he joked, his voice quiet as he looked at her.

Olivia didn't laugh. She just stared blankly at the azure sky, watching a large dark bird circle overhead, its wide wings outstretched as it glided smoothly on the warm air currents.

'Have you told him?' Greg asked suddenly. His eyes traced hers with a frown. 'About us? That we're not getting married?'

'No.' She kept her eyes on the bird overhead. It reminded her of Nick; predatory, dangerous—just waiting for a chance to kill. 'Like a thunderbolt, he falls . . .' she said softly, and her eyes narrowed.

Greg followed her gaze. 'Yes,' he murmured, recognising the quote from Tennyson. He watched the dark bird for a moment. 'He does remind me of Nick,' he said softly, turning back to Olivia with a shudder.

Olivia sighed, dropping her gaze. She traced patterns in the bleached yellow grass. It crackled beneath her fingertips and she watched it without expression, wondering when Nick would get home. Pretty soon, she realised, looking at her watch. It was nearly seven-thirty.

Greg's eyes were gentle. 'You've really got it bad, haven't you?' he said quietly, and she heard the sympathy in his voice.

She didn't answer. Yes, she thought, I've really got it bad. She sighed, raising her brows, and stared across the garden to the house. It stared back at her, a powerful stone edifice, impenetrable.

Greg slowly got to his feet, thrusting his hands in his

pockets. 'Simonetta's taking me to the village,' he said hesitantly, and watched her with a frown. 'I think I have to leave now. We're visiting some friends there.'

Olivia looked up, her eyes blank for a moment. Then she smiled and stood up too, brushing grass from her skirt. 'You'd better go, then, hadn't you?'

'Well ...' he shifted uncertainly, kicking the dusty ground at his feet, looking at her with a troubled face.

She smiled. 'Go on,' she told him, giving him a little nudge, 'she'll be waiting for you.' She tilted her head when he still didn't move. 'She won't wait for ever, you know!'

Greg watched her with thoughtful eyes in silence for a moment. 'No,' he said slowly, and his eyes narrowed suddenly. A slow smile dawned on his face. 'You're right,' he said quietly, 'she won't wait for ever.'

She took his hand, her eyes affectionate as she smiled at him. 'You're very slow, Greg,' she said quietly, then grinned. 'But you get there eventually!'

He watched her with a little smile, his expression sheepish. Then he grinned. 'You're a kind girl,' he said curiously. On an impulse he took her face in his hands and bent to kiss her mouth gently. 'Good luck,' he said softly, squeezing her hands before turning to walk to the gates.

She watched him go. Why didn't I fall in love with Greg? she asked herself irritably.

She turned away, beginning to walk back to the house. It was then that she saw him. Nick stood by the dark car in the drive, his eyes narrowed as he watched her walk towards him. Her step faltered momentarily, but she felt her heart lift and quickened her step, feeling slightly breathless as she reached him.

'Hallo,' she said with a bright smile, her eyes intense as she watched him. She couldn't risk letting him guess exactly how she felt. She wanted to tell him she wasn't marrying Greg, but after that she would keep herself firmly in check.

Nick gave her a slow, tight smile. 'A touching scene,' he drawled, and his eyes flicked over her. 'Poor Olivia, I don't suppose you like having the tables turned on you.'

A frown pulled her brows together. 'You don't understand,' she began, watching him.

'I understand perfectly,' he said, and raised one brow. 'You're lonely because Greg's with Simonetta.' He shrugged, his shoulders powerful beneath his dark suit. 'Simonetta today—you tomorrow. Nice arrangement. I wouldn't mind a set-up like that myself.'

'There is no set-up,' she told him coolly, keeping her face firmly controlled. She watched him for a moment, her body tense. 'Nick—Greg and I are finished. We're not getting married.' She studied his dark face. 'It's over.'

There was a long silence. She could feel the heat of his gaze on her, his body motionless as he just stared at her. His lashes flickered against his cheek as he watched her.

He was totally still. 'I suppose you'll be leaving, then,' he said expressionlessly.

'I suppose so.' Olivia prayed he would ask her to stay, but there was no way she would ask him. The fear of rejection was more than her already battered pride could take.

Nick shrugged, avoiding her eyes. He looked away across the garden. 'There's nothing to keep you here,' he said in a flat, expressionless voice, 'Is there?'

She heard the words in a tidal wave of shock. She had thought he at least cared for her a little. She stared at him bleakly, all vestiges of hope torn apart, wishing she could somehow tell him how she felt without making a fool of herself. But it couldn't be done.

She bent her head to disguise the pain in her eyes. 'No,' she said under her breath, 'I suppose you're right.' Her heart winced and she gave a bitter forced smile. 'There's nothing to keep me here.'

Nick was motionless, his features harsh, brooding as he studied her bent head. The silence was unbearable. The insects buzzed and danced around them, invisible in the warm still garden.

'I'm glad you agree,' Nick said in a flat tone.

Olivia slowly raised her head. 'When can I leave?' She thought her voice might crack, give her away, but it remained steady, even though she was aching inside.

His eyes leapt with anger. 'I don't give a damn when you leave!' he said tightly. 'Ring the airport whenever you like! Tonino will drive you.'

Her mouth tightened with pain and anger. 'Thanks a lot!' she snapped, her eyes burning with resentment. She could feel tears stinging her eyes, her throat closing up. 'You just can't wait to see the back of me, can you?'

'No,' he said between tightly clenched teeth, 'the sooner you leave the better.'

He stared at her for one vividly angry moment, then turned on his heel and strode into the house, leaving her standing alone on the driveway. She wanted to cry, but instead she kicked her feet restlessly in the dust, watching blankly as the creamy white clouds spilled from her toes. She compressed her lips. He doesn't care, she thought bitterly. He never did. I was just kidding myself.

She walked into the house, the set of her shoulders defeated, lonely.

CHAPTER TEN

SHE rang the airport the next day. Booking the Palermo–Rome, Rome–London flight held a finality which made her feel totally empty. I'm really leaving, she thought as she put the telephone back in its cradle. The bell rang once into the silence as she replaced the receiver, echoing in the stark hall.

Inside she felt numb, anaesthetised, as though what was happening wasn't real. It seemed incredible that within twenty-four hours she would be removed from Nick's side for ever. Slowly she went upstairs and packed her cases, her face white and blank as she did so.

A knock at the door brought her head up. 'Come in,' she said shakily, and her heart leapt as the door pushed back and Nick came in.

The grey eyes flicked to her cases on the bed. 'When are you leaving?' he asked in an expressionless voice.

'Tonight.' She could barely force the word out, her eyes intent on his face as she stood totally rigid, her heart thudding painfully inside her, just watching him, drinking in every detail of his face.

Nick was staring at her. 'I didn't think it would be so soon,' he said, and thrust his hands into his pockets, watching her. There was a long intense silence, then he took a step forwards. 'Olivia, I . . .' he broke off abruptly, turning away. 'Never mind.'

'No, wait!' She forced herself to move, going over to him, her eyes wide with a flare of hope. 'What were you going to say?'

He flicked his eyes over her, his face harsh. 'It doesn't matter,' he said in a clipped voice. He gave her a tight smile. 'Have a good flight.'

Olivia stood watching as he closed the door, leaving her alone in the deathly silence, her heart constricting painfully. She closed her eyes on a spasm of pain, linking her hands together. He really doesn't give a damn, she thought bitterly.

It was nearly eleven before she ventured outside her room again. Going downstairs, she looked around vaguely for a sign of life, but as far as she could see, everyone was out. She went into the kitchen, expecting to find Lala hovering over the stove, but the room was empty. Sighing, she closed the door and went into the garden.

It was unbearably hot. The sun scorched the back of her head, turning her hair into glistening black threads which burned at the touch. Insects danced crazily beneath the lush green shrubs around the grey-bleached stone walls of the Palazzo Baretta.

As she wandered towards the stone gates she thought driftingly of taking a walk. Nick had made it clear that the villagers now knew who she was, and wouldn't attack her again. Perhaps it would be safe, just to walk a little way.

The roads were dusty, a creamy grey, banked on either side by scorched grass, fragrant pink flowers and lush green shrubs. Olivia walked slowly, breathing in the hot, lazy atmosphere.

The sound of a car engine made her frown. She

turned, her eyes screwed up against the glare of the sun. A long black car crawled towards her, glittering in the sunlight, its wheels sending up clouds of dust.

The car stopped close to her. The chrome flashed as the car door opened.

'Miss Courtney.' The man Scaletta's soft voice made her stiffen, icy chills ran down her spine.

'Hello.' She moistened her suddenly dry lips, eyeing him warily, her whole body tensed with dislike.

Scaletta smiled, and her flesh crawled uneasily. 'What a pleasant surprise,' he said softly, and she saw his glistening white teeth flash as he came towards her. 'Can I offer you a lift?'

Olivia swallowed, her throat parched. 'I was just going back to the house,' she said quietly, watching him.

Scaletta's hand slid on to her arm like a slippery eel. 'On such a beautiful day?' He smiled again, drawing her towards the car. 'You are heartless. It isn't often that I get the chance to spend time with a beautiful lady.'

I can understand why, thought Olivia, feeling sick. She gave him a frightened smile, then said, 'Mr Baretta will wonder where I am.'

Scaletta's smile disappeared. He stopped, turning his head slowly, and the dead black eyes ran over her. 'Pulling rank?' he asked softly.

'No.' She shook her head, swallowing. Her stomach was clenched tightly, beads of perspiration breaking out on her forehead like dew.

He watched her for a long, unnerving moment. His lifeless eyes sent chills of dislike through her, and she thought once again of the dead fish he reminded her of. Then he smiled, frightening her even more.

'Good,' he murmured, opening the car door and propelling her inside. He walked to the other side, and slipped in beside her. 'We shall drive together for a while,' he told her softly as he started the engine.

Olivia edged close to the door as they pulled smoothly away, clouds of dust shimmering from the wheels. Her eyes were wide in her face, her skin white, dewed with perspiration. Why did I come outside the Palazzo gardens? she asked herself desperately. I should have stayed where I was.

They sped past acres of bleached grass, hilltops of lush green with sheep grazing, tended by young men in black. Bright splashes of pink dotted the land where flowers grew and flourished. The sky was a dazzling azure blue, the land a sprawling, wild terrain of bright greens and yellows.

Olivia looked round sharply as the car stopped. They were to one side of the road, partially hidden by a clump of trees.

'This is where we stop,' Scaletta said softly, leaning back in his seat.

Olivia moistened her parched lips. 'Where are we?' she asked, looking around at the rough, bare field next to them.

He smiled. 'Not far from Solunto,' he told her. He studied her in a tense, unpleasant silence, then one hand reached out like a cobra to touch her hair. 'Beautiful,' he murmured, stroking it with long, dark fingers.

Olivia's stomach knotted with dislike. 'Please!' She brushed his hand away tentatively, unwilling to risk offending him by being brusque.

He ignored her. 'Your eyes fascinate me,' he said softly, 'So blue. They remind me of a Sicilian sky in summer.' He smiled again, spreading his hands. 'You see? I am a romantic.' He raised his thick dark brows slowly, tilting his black head. 'Are you a romantic?'

She gave him a taut smile. 'Aren't most women?' she countered, wanting to jump out of the car and run as far as she possibly could away from him.

'Unfortunately, no.' He watched her with those lifeless black eyes for a moment. 'Some women are realists—hard-headed.' His long fingers stroked the side of her cheek and Olivia tried not to pull away in distaste. 'But I can see you aren't hard-headed.' His fingers trailed to her mouth. 'Or you wouldn't be in love with Nick Barctta.'

She stiffened. 'I'm not,' she said through tight, dry lips.

Scaletta laughed softly, and Olivia felt sick to her stomach. 'You are,' he said in a chilling, quiet voice. He raised his brows. 'Is he in love with you?'

She thought quickly. If she said yes, Scaletta would have a powerful club to wield over Nick, but it might also make him leave her alone. She moistened her lips. 'Yes,' she said, wishing it was true, 'Nick loves me.' Scaletta must know how violent Nick was, she reasoned, he would surely leave her alone now.

Scaletta's smile disappeared. 'Good,' he said, and the black lifeless eyes made her eyes widen in fear. He started the car engine again, reversing it quickly while Olivia stared at him in sudden apprehension.

'Are we going back now?' she asked shakily as he put the car in gear.

Scaletta turned to her slowly. 'We are going to my home,' he said, and a slow, unpleasant smile touched his lips.

Another car screamed around the corner. The wheels

skidded, dust throwing up around them. It screeched to a lurching halt in front of Scaletta's car, stopping him from driving on.

Olivia's heart leapt as she saw Nick jump out of the car, his face tight with anger. He came over to them and wrenched the car door open, looking down at them.

'What the hell are you doing?' Nick asked under his breath, his teeth clenched tightly together.

Scaletta looked at him with cold hatred, then he smiled. 'I was having a charming conversation,' he said sneeringly, and indicated Olivia, 'with your mistress.'

Nick's eyes flashed with rage and a muscle jerked in his cheek. 'Get out of that car,' he said dangerously.

Scaletta's brows rose. 'And disappoint the lady? She was just about to add another lover to her list of conquests.'

Nick's face was murderous. 'You bastard!' he ground out. Then he lunged forward, wrenching Scaletta out of the car in one jerky movement.

His fist shot out and cracked Scaletta on the jaw, sending him flying backwards to land flat on the road. Nick went after him, his eyes filled with burning anger. His lips drew back from his teeth in a snarl of animal rage. He hauled Scaletta up by his collar, throwing another lethal punch that sent the man spinning, a crack of bone splintering through the air as he landed with a thud on his back.

Nick looked down at him, breathing harshly. 'Go anywhere near her again,' he grated through his teeth, 'and I'll kill you!'

He turned on his heel and came back to the car. Olivia stood on the road, watching, her face filled with horror. Scaletta was sprawled on his back, groaning, his hand moving sluggishly to rub his broken jaw. Nick came towards her.

'How did you know?' Olivia whispered as he stood by the car with her.

'Tonino saw you,' said Nick, his breathing ragged. He watched her for a long moment, then asked tightly, 'Why did you get in the car with him? Are you stupid?'

She bit her lip. 'He frightens me,' she said quietly.

He slammed his hand on the roof of the car. '*Goddamn it!*' he shouted angrily. 'You should have . . .' he broke off abruptly, his mouth tightening. He looked away.

Olivia watched the back of his black head. He rested his hands on the roof of the car, looking away from her, his dark face tight with anger, his cheek jerking as he controlled his temper.

'I'm sorry,' she said sadly, her eyes stinging with tears. It wasn't fair. She had been too scared to refuse to get in the car. If she'd known Tonino was nearby she would have run like blazes the minute she saw him.

She looked back at Nick's angry face, turned away from her. 'Why were you so angry?' she asked in a half whisper.

Nick stared fixedly at his hands on the roof of the car. His face was rigid, a muscle jerking wildly under the dark skin. She saw the back of his neck redden as he stood in total silence, then he turned his head slowly but didn't look at her, his eyes avoiding hers, a stain of red running along his angular cheekbone. Then his gaze flicked to hers and she saw his heart in his eyes, the mask stripped away, his feelings laid bare for a few precious seconds.

'I love you,' he said hoarsely.

Her heart thumped violently, and she stared at him, feeling her knees weaken, rendered totally speechless. Then she moved, slowly at first until she was only a few steps away from him.

'I want you to stay,' Nick said in a raw voice. He looked away, and kicked the wheel of the car, his body tense. 'But you don't have to.'

Olivia was too choked up to speak. She felt herself begin to tremble, and moved closer to him. 'I'll stay,' she said shakily.

Nick looked round, staring at her fixedly. 'For how long?' he asked, his body rigid.

She managed a tremulous smile, her vision blurring with tears of joy. 'For as long as you want me,' she said huskily.

His grey eyes burned into her with raw emotion. 'That's going to be a long time,' he said deeply, and his voice was hesitant, as though he was feeling his way, afraid that the ground would give way beneath him. 'How do you know you'll want to stay that long.'

There was a little silence. Then she said huskily, 'Because I love you.'

He stared at her for a moment in shocked disbelief. Then he swept her into his arms, crushing her against him with a deep groan, his hands pressing her tightly, his body relaxing as he breathed out with relief.

'I've been taking risks all my life,' he said deeply, and his fingers stroked her hair as he pressed her face into his shoulder, clinging to her, 'but this is the first time I was actually scared I'd lose the gamble.'

Olivia felt herself shiver. 'We both nearly lost,' she said quietly, and tightened her hands on his shoulders, afraid for both of them. They had so very nearly lost each other through pride and fear. How stupid, she thought, closing her eyes. We would have walked away from each other because we were both too scared to say how we felt.

'How long have you known?' Nick asked suddenly, drawing away to look down at her intently. 'When did you start loving me?'

Her eyes met his. 'I don't know,' she said, her pulses leaping at the emotion she saw in his eyes. 'I think I started loving you before I even realised it.'

'I fell in love with you the moment I saw you,' he said deeply, and his face softened as he smiled tenderly at her amazed expression. 'Why do you think I didn't say anything when I came to your house in London?'

She ran a hand over his face, tracing the harsh, aggressive lines of cheek and jaw. 'I thought you were just trying to frighten me.'

'Frighten you?' He was amazed, shaking his head. 'My God! If only you knew how I felt! It was like being kicked in the teeth. I couldn't speak, I just kept staring at you and wondering why the hell this was happening to me. I thought God was playing some terrible joke on me.'

There was a loud bang as Scaletta got into his car, slamming the door behind him. They both watched as the engine roared, and he drove away at top speed, clouds of dust billowing out after him.

'That's the last we'll see of him,' Nick said tightly, and she saw his eyes flash. 'The little bastard! I wanted to kill him.'

Olivia frowned, pulling away for a moment. 'You're so violent,' she said in a hushed, anxious voice. 'You frighten me.'

He looked at her, startled. 'Darling, I've never been violent with you.' He grimaced, reddening a little. 'It may have seemed that way—but that was because I was scared as hell. My feelings were running away from me, I just couldn't control them. I lashed out in self-defence at whatever was causing it.' He gave her a crooked smile. 'I guess I just couldn't cope.'

Olivia relaxed in the circle of his arms. 'I know the feeling,' she murmured, looking up with a teasing smile, her eyes twinkling. 'You had a pretty powerful effect on me too!'

Nick watched her in silence for a long moment. His eyes were intent on her face.

'Marry me,' he said deeply.

She frowned, her eyes worried. 'We're so different, Nick.' Their families, their backgrounds were so far apart it might cause trouble between them in marriage.

He clasped her hand to his chest. 'What's so different?' he demanded as they both felt the violent thud of his heart. 'Marry me,' he said again, with urgency. 'Go where your feelings take you. I'm not letting you go just because my parents are Sicilian and yours are English.'

She looked at him with affectionate irritation. 'Don't rush me, Nick,' she said, her cheeks dimpling, 'You're like a hurricane—you just whirl around, destroying opposition. Stop knocking me breathless!'

'Not until you say you'll marry me,' he said obstinately.

She laughed, shaking her head. 'You're impossible!'

'Totally,' Nick agreed, smiling, and bent his head to kiss her until she clung to him.

THE MAN WITH THE GOLDEN TOUCH

Many of the myths and legends of ancient Greece are stories with morals. Some are rather light and humorous, particularly the Dionysiac legends, which are tales revolving around Dionysus, the god of wine. The most famous of these is the story of King Midas, a ruler of ancient Phrygia.

One day, King Midas caught a satyr in his garden; this particular satyr was one of Dionysus's protectors. Midas was a good-natured king and treated his captive well. When Dionysus came to collect the errant satyr he rewarded Midas with a wish. Without thinking of the dreadful consequences, Midas wished that all he touched might turn to gold. How thrilled he was as he passed through his palace, turning his furniture and statues into gold—and quickly becoming extremely wealthy!

His problems began, however, when he sat down to eat, because the food he picked up turned to gold as soon as it touched his mouth. Poor King Midas almost starved to death! Dionysus, laughing merrily at Midas's foolishness, granted him release if he bathed in a certain river—and to this day that river is known to contain traces of gold in its water.

Perhaps this old story is meant to serve as a warning about the oft-dire consequences of greed. But today, when someone is said to have the ''Midas touch'' or is said to be ''a walking Midas,'' as Nick Baretta is in Sarah Holland's book, it usually means that he is an excellent businessman, for whom all ventures turn out financially successful!

What readers say about SUPERROMANCE

SUPERROMANCE

Longer, exciting, sensuous and dramatic!

Fascinating love stories that will hold you in their magical spell till the last page is turned!

Now's your chance to discover the earlier books in this exciting series. Choose from the great selection on the following page!

Choose from this list of great
SUPERROMANCES!

SUPERROMANCE

Complete and mail this coupon today!

Worldwide Reader Service

In the U.S.A.
1440 South Priest Drive
Tempe, AZ 85281

In Canada
649 Ontario Street
Stratford, Ontario N5A 6W2

Please send me the following SUPERROMANCES. I am enclosing my
check or money order for $2.50 for each copy ordered, plus 75¢ to
cover postage and handling.

☐ # 8   ☐ # 14   ☐ # 20
☐ # 9   ☐ # 15   ☐ # 21
☐ # 10   ☐ # 16   ☐ # 22
☐ # 11   ☐ # 17   ☐ # 23
☐ # 12   ☐ # 18   ☐ # 24
☐ # 13   ☐ # 19   ☐ # 25

Number of copies checked @ $2.50 each = $_____
N.Y. and Ariz. residents add appropriate sales tax $_____
Postage and handling $____.75

                    TOTAL $_____

I enclose_____.
(Please send check or money order. We cannot be responsible for cash
sent through the mail.)
Prices subject to change without notice.

NAME_____
                 (Please Print)
ADDRESS_____APT. NO._____
CITY_____
STATE/PROV._____
ZIP/POSTAL CODE_____

Offer expires September 30, 1983   3035600000